FINAL VENGEANCE

ARTHUR CRANDON

Arthur Crandon Publishing
22nd Floor Hing Bong Commercial Building Wanchai, Hong Kong
www.arthurcrandon.com

Publisher's Note: This is a work of fiction. Names, characters, places, and
incidents are a product of the author's imagination. Locales and public names
are sometimes used for atmospheric purposes. Any resemblance to actual
people, living or dead, or to businesses, companies, events, institutions, or
locales is completely coincidental.

ISBN: 978-1-9161408-6-8

Acknowledgements

My writing journey has brought me to this, my third book written about the Philippines. I hope readers will enjoy learning about the pleasures and the pitfalls of these beautiful islands.

If you spend any time there you will soon realize that not all is as it seems.

Beneath the friendly and welcoming surface there is a culture of criminality and deceit as is common in third world countries.

I want to thank my many Philippino friends, in The Philippines, Hong Kong, and the U.K., who have assisted me with research and anecdotes which have helped me to put together a work which, I hope, will open your eyes to the reality of these exotic lands.

TABLE OF CONTENTS

ONE

Home Alone

The tired old soldier snored and moved restlessly. He looked like a vagrant. Paul McCain did not sleep well. Even after so many years, he couldn't get the sound of exploding mortar shells out of his ears; the vibration shook his head, making him faint.

Nothing like it existed in what he now called real life, but this appeared real to him as well. Over time, it got better. Days seemed mostly okay, but not the nights.

He had the back seat to himself, so he stretched out; but the jolting and shaking was worse there and he never slept well.

The time between sleeping and waking – they call it REM sleep – is where the nightmares live. Now was such a time.

He'd been travelling now for many hours and his body knew they werenearing their destination. It was time to wake. His eyelids fluttered, he could see that it was dawn.

The rickety old bus juddered and jerked as it made its way north through the receding darkness from Manila. He was unlucky tonight. It was one of the older ones. It had dirty, damaged seats, cracked windows, and no air conditioning.

Paul always travelled during the night; it was quieter and faster. By day, the trip took more than fifteen hours. He usually slept, despite the potholes, the grinding screech of the brakes, and frequent toilet and snack stops; and, of course, the nightmares.

They were not really nightmares, more like memories, but distorted, magnified. The past coming back to haunt him, resurrecting the pain, the turmoil, the fear. They always left him with the worst despair.

Today began no differently. He pushed the images and the ragged emotions from his mind. The sun appeared over the Cordillera mountains on his right and the temperature started to rise. He gradually realized he was no longer in Helmand. He was safe, but he knew the fear, the anguish, the despair would stay with him until he forced them away with the events of the dawn.

For the past few weeks, there had been fresh horrors to face, displacing the ghosts of his time in Afghanistan. These horrors were worse; they did not fade when he woke up.

He was nearly sixty, and a fool. For years he took his gorgeous young wife for granted, and neglected their twelve-year-old son, Dennis. The lies, the women, the gambling…

Being sorry did not help now, it was too late, his family were gone. Never the best family man, he'd broken every marital vow, and then some, but he missed his wife and son now, so much.

His long-suffering wife, Editha lived in another country with his son, and her new lover. He remembered every detail of the call he got from her as she waited for the plane to take her out of the country, taking Dennis with her. She said she would not stop him having contact with Dennis, but he had not heard from her for four weeks now. The heartache bore down like a dark cloud, crushing him. His phone never left his side just in case she rang.

On better days he planned that they would one day get back together, and he would be the husband and father he should always have been. Today was not one of those days.

He would be home in three hours. Should he call it home? He arrived back for the first time in many weeks to an empty house. When he last left, they were a family, a father and mother taking their son to school. So much had happened since then, but in his mind, he remembered the three of them smiling as they left, not knowing what tumultuous events would later unfold.

He'd planned everything so well – by now he and his family would have no cares, lots of money, a carefree life, but his attempt to blackmail the politician failed.

The wily senator promised to give him a fortune to keep quiet about what the corrupt mans crimes, but Senator Consuelo died from food poisoning without paying.

Paul left Manila with little money, just what he got from selling the photos and a few television interviews. Nothing else.

He had to move forward; he was a Marine – that was central to him. it gave him stability in this mean and unreliable world.

Despite his sadness, he would pull through. His training at least provided him that; he had to battle on. One day he would be with his lovely son again and he wanted the lad to be proud of him.

After dozing fitfully for a couple more hours. he opened his eyes to the familiar landscape of his home province. The bus slowed down now.

His house loomed ahead on the left. It stopped nearly at the gate. The substantial detached building occupied a stretch of land between the road and the beach.

The months of neglect showed. Paint flaked off the walls, and weeds shot up in the cracks in the drive. The once immaculately laid lawns had become brown and patchy from the intense heat and lack of water. Seed spikes stuck up and surviving grass clustered in untidy, uneven tufts. It had not been mown for ages. The weeds sprouting all over were knee high now. Flower beds were becoming overrun with weeds and dead leaves covered the driveway. Usually, his first job in the morning was to sweep the yard. He wouldn't bother today. No point anymore. Prospective buyers could take it as it was, or leave it.

He built the imposing structure for his wife when he left the army and moved to the Philippines. Despite his age he laboured every day with the local builders and did twice as much work as the other men.

Editha seemed happy at that time, or so he thought. His son Dennis had known no other home, until now. His mind wandered to where Editha and Dennis might be.

Paul left the service a long while ago, honourable discharge, of course. He missed the three stripes; he used to get respect. Civilian life did not suit him, but he'd tried to make a go of it. Tall and slim, and with his dyed black hair, he didn't look his age, often passing for being much younger.

The rusty black wrought ironwork gate creaked as he swung it open. He had been meaning to oil it for months before he left; today, he didn't care.

He had a heavy heart, seeing the house it a dilapidated state. Good memories had become eclipsed by the hole inside him, the gnawing emptiness. He hoped he would hear from her soon, but as the days wore on, he became sullen and resigned to the new norm - life as a single man, and an old man at that.

On one of his good days last week he'd decided to take positive steps. He would leave Manila. The capital city held no prospects for him. First, he would sell the house and use the money to make a fresh start, and he would ask around the neighbours, someone might be in contact with his family.

Of course, the dwelling had been bought in his wife's name. The law in the Philippines meant that foreigners may not own land. But when they registered it, he'd made her pre-sign a set of sale and transfer documents, just in case. The mistrust hurt her, but he didn't care about her feelings then.

***

Better get a move on, he thought, looking at his watch. He fought the gloom. He had to be motivated today. Despite his earlier mood he wanted the place to look it's best. After a coffee he set about the cleaning, tidying, watering the plants etc. His realtor friend, Monique, would come by soon after lunch with prospective buyers. He even tackled the piles of leaves in the porch and driveway; Paul needed to sell this house, and it had to be today.

He would not stay here. If it did not sell today, he would find a cheap hotel until it did. Divorce papers had arrived a couple of months ago, at least that's what he presumed the fat envelope contained. He hadn't faced opening it yet. Whatever she would do, she'd have to do it without his help.

Everything in the refrigerator was stale, but he found some cans and made beans on toast; he'd had the foresight to buy bread before leaving Manila. The freezer was nearly empty, but what remained he put in a refuse sack and left at the top of the drive. He would give a set of keys to Monique this afternoon. Tomorrow morning, if all as he hoped, he would be on his way to Angeles, and would not be coming back.

He made coffee; Monique told him too – the smell of coffee would be welcoming. He just finished when he saw the outlines of his approaching visitors through the glass door before they rang the bell. Two o'clock; Monique was on time, he liked that about her. As he opened the door, she greeted him like an old friend.

"Hello Paul, how are you? It's been a long time."

She gave him the briefest of hugs, her eyes already sizing up the property.

"Yes, I guess it's been a while. I've been away a lot. Time goes so quickly."

Paul looked expectantly at Monique; it was time for introductions.

"Paul, this is Eddie and Sue Jameson. Sue is a local girl. She met Eddie online a couple of years ago. He's Australian."

The burly Aussie smiled as he leaned forward to shake Paul's hand. His grip was firm. Paul had him sized up in a second. A late middle-aged, overweight man with a thing for young Asian girls.

"Were you in the forces, Eddie?" Paul already knew the answer but thought he should make conversation.

"Nah. Mate. Farmer me, all my life, and my dad and grandpa before me. Cattle. Best beef stock in Northern Australia. I'll be retiring soon and we're looking for a place to spend more time here in the Province, my son will carry on the proud tradition back home." He looked down at his wife.

"Her folks live just up the road."

"This place should be just right for you, then, Eddie."

Paul led them into the house and towards the stairs.

"I'll let Monique show you around, then we can chat later."

As they turned away, he lost the false smile he'd been holding for too long. He'd forced himself to be pleasant, it wasn't easy; but if these guys came up with the price, they could have the place, furniture, and all.

Back in the kitchen he turned off the coffee machine, it had done its job, and made a cup with the final dregs. Through the window the garden looked fresh from his watering. The tomatoes did not look well – they needed constant attention, and now they sat in sorry rows together with the beans, onions, and bitter melons.

He used to do the big jobs, the mowing, the leaves, etc. but this had been Editha's garden, tended faithfully every day; she'd just abandoned it for her new life, whatever that may be.

He heard noises from above. They slowly came down the polished wooden stairs, Sue's heels clicked on each step. Animated discussions with Monique sounded positive. His smile resurfaced.

"You've got a delightful place here, mate. Why d'you want to sell it?"

"Personal reasons," said Paul, still maintaining his smile.

Monique came to the rescue.

"Paul's suffered a bereavement and needs to move away."

"Oh, I see. Sorry mate, I didn't mean to pry."

"That's fine, don't worry about it, we all have our cross to bear. Anyway, did you like the house?"

"It's just what we need, mate. The only thing is we need it quickly. We're staying in hotels every time we come here and it's getting expensive. When will it be vacant and free?"

Paul wanted to say *about 30 minutes after you leave,* but thought better of it – that would provoke further questions which he didn't want to answer.

"Is the end of the month okay?"

It was only 10 days – it seemed a reasonable gap.

"Well that will be fine, I think we have a deal. I don't want to haggle with you, you seem a nice fella. We can give Monique a deposit today, and we'll pay the full asking price, if it includes all the furniture and appliances. Is that ok with you?" Paul smiled again, in agreement.

"I'll leave Monique to sort out the paperwork and as soon as the money is paid, she can release the keys to you." He made a show of passing the keys to the happy realtor.

Eddie beamed and shot out his hand again. Paul grasped it and returned the handshake. "I hope you'll be very happy here," said Paul, hoping they would leave soon.

He wasn't disappointed. Minutes later, he watched them drive away.

As their car disappeared down the dusty road Paul prepared to leave.

He took all he wanted – clothes, a few mementos, a photo album – he piled everything into the boot and backseat of his car, he'd bought a new Toyota Prius in Manila – it took half his money, but at least he had transport now.

The clock on the wall in the kitchen still worked, it was nearly three o'clock – it would start to get dark soon. He realized there was nothing to stay for now, nothing to stop him leaving. Why wait any longer? He smiled for real, the pressure lifted. He didn't have to spend a night there – if he didn't waste time, he would be in Angeles before dark.

Leaving the house for the last time, he noticed the red, wooden, letter box attached to the front door. You had to open the top to see any letters. He did not expect anything, but he thought he'd check it anyway. The cover, swollen from the recent rains, creaked open, then he saw it - a white envelope addressed to him in Editha's handwriting. Suddenly, his mood changed, and the smile disappeared.

With an unsteady hand, he tore it open.

Dear Paul,

I am sorry it has taken me so long to contact you, but there has been a lot to do and I've had to be very careful. People have been trying to find me because of that Consuelo business and your involvement. We had to leave the country Paul. It might be dangerous for us to be there.

He paused and looked at the postmark – Manila, Philippines. As if to answer his question, the letter continued:

I can't tell you where we are now, so I sent this to a friend who posted it on to you. Anyway, I hope you are getting yourself together. I am happy now, happier than in a long time, and there will never be any hope for us as a family (if we ever were that). But I will keep my word, I will not stop you seeing Dennis, it is just that now is not the right time. You will have to wait. I'll contact you again when things are more settled. I won't give you any contact details now. I know you won't like it, but I'm not too concerned with what you like now Paul. I have the strength not to let you hurt me.

I want nothing from you Paul, you can keep your money, the house, everything. We will not be needing it.

Dennis is fine, and, of course, he misses you. I'm sure in the future you can get to know him again. He is a great kid.Editha.

He sat in the car and re-read the letter four times, before driving off. Was he really such a terrible husband and father to deserve such treatment? On reflection, and with dismay, he realized that he probably was. He would give anything to have the opportunity to make it up to his long-suffering family, but he would never get the chance now.

Editha did not have money of her own, he was too mean to let her save any, and he knew her family were not wealthy. Why doesn't she need money? The thought crept into his head, but he already knew the answer. She had someone else now. How could she? His blood rose; self-control was not one of Paul's strengths. Automatically, he started the training his counsellor had taught him. Deep breaths, controlled breathing, counting slowly to four. After a few minutes, the thunder clouds passed.

His Marine skills also kicked in. If you can't do anything about it, don't worry about it. Pick yourself up, dust yourself off and make the best of it. Tears welled in the corner of his eyes as he set off for Angeles City.

After two hours on the dusty road, he stopped for a coffee. The large, red, Jollibee seemed quiet, not too crowded – there were only a few cars in the carpark, and at least you knew the coffee would not be dreadful.

Jollibee had become the largest fast-food chain in the Philippines, focusing on chicken and rice, the large hoardings with the jolly 'bee' neon sign grinned at you as you approached. As he glanced around, he saw that the customers were mostly young families, or businessmen passing through. He suddenly felt alone. He wondered how long it would take before he would feel better.

The breeze of the late afternoon cooled the air a little, but the sun would continue to beat down for a while before the still of the evening took over.

The perilous mountain roads from Benguet often collapsed with heavy rains. Many coaches and cars tipped over into the valleys below each year, causing many deaths. Paul knew the road well. he was used to the twists and turns, soon he approached the major road. From a distance he could see the cars and lorries moving along like ants. He joined up with them at San Fernando.

The Northern Luzon Express way became just a two-lane road at this point. It would widen out to four then six lanes past Angeles, but he would not be going that far.

The trip to Angeles City excited him, his first 'adventure' since the breakup and all the issues in Manila, but he had mixed feelings. The pain in his heart was still there, but he now also had the prospect of something new, the anticipation of a fresh start.

It was in Angeles that he'd met Editha all those years ago. She worked in a bar. Like most of the working girls there she dreamed of finding a foreign husband.

The night Paul walked into her bar she had just split up with Greg, a long-term boyfriend, and U.S. Army major. He'd been careless and left his phone unattended when he needed the toilet. The pictures of his wife and two children she'd found were difficult to explain away, although he'd tried. He had told her he wasn't married.

Greg was not a great catch. He was short, and bald, but at least he might get her to the U.S. - the land of opportunity, or so she thought.

So, Paul caught her on the re-bound. A U.S. Marine; a real catch. They got married within the year, but she failed to get a visa to join Paul in America. – Paul lied about some drug offenses in his youth, and the immigration authorities declined her application, so he decided he would come and live with her here in the Philippines. She'd been a nearly perfect wife and mother, but Paul's behaviour had damaged their marriage over the years. She'd tolerated the other women, so long as he came home to her, but he showed little interest in their son, Dennis.

The boy adored his father, and it broke Editha's heart to see how Paul ignored him. But while he supported them financially; Editha would not rock the boat.

In the three years he lived in Angeles earlier he came to know the city very well. So today was like coming home in a way, but he would avoid the area and the bar where he met Editha – he was not ready for that yet. Taking the escape road towards Angeles and Olongopo he could see the familiar skyline two or three kilometers down the road, He was approaching the city now. The lights of the metropolis glowed in the distance.

Rice paddies, tobacco fields, small farms appeared along either side of the road and stretched into the hazy distance. Run-down shacks selling chips and soda, and occasionally gasoline became more frequent now. As he neared the municipality, they gave way to more substantial buildings, gas stations and eateries. There was a small hotel close to the centre; he'd been a regular there in the old days. Since the American soldiers left, the place was not so busy, but he hoped to find a veteran or two there. They would probably be younger than him – he wouldn't know them – he hoped. There were old friends he would look up when he was up to it, but for now, he would take things slowly.

As he drove through the familiar streets, he started to feel a little better, stronger. Everything will be better – it will just take time. Suddenly, it loomed ahead. Newly painted, but unmistakably the same place, the Blue Room.

A group of young local lads sat around a square wooden table beside the white double doors. They'd just started on their Red Horse beers, laughing, and joking; they would enjoy a happy evening. As he locked his car outside, the light dimmed, and the streetlights turned on, illuminating the street scene and the rowdy youths.

They quieted as Paul passed them. Local lads respected the U.S. army, and they assumed any American they met would likely be a U.S. vet., it was safer that way. Most active service guys left the city a long time ago. The Philippine Government asked them to go after an incident involving a GI and a local girl. It was the wrong decision. The entire country suffered from their departure; they spent a lot of money, and they helped to keep law and order.

Official military troops had mostly left, but many of them quit the service or retired and stayed behind. Some of them married local girls. Angeles city boasted a large, but aging, expat veteran community.

The Blue Room Hotel seemed just as Paul remembered it. Recessed from the road. With parking spaces at the side, there was room for a few tables and chairs in the front. Blue and white, the painted walls were just as he recalled.

The striking colours stood out in an otherwise drab and run-down street. Perhaps the same owners were still there. If not, the new people obviously kept the same colour scheme. Between the tables on the pavement was a doorway. Not a grand entrance. Just a simple wooden door.

It was like going back in time. The place hadn't changed in the fifteen years he'd been away. Girls were busy behind the bar/reception on the left and a big old American style fan whirred noisily in the centre of the ceiling above. He was sure that the tables and chairs were the same, his military training had given him an eye for detail and an excellent memory.

Pleasant smells of beer, and food cooking in the kitchen wafted through and brought back memories. The old pool table was still in the corner, but the beer stains were gone – It looked like they had recovered it. On the right, the entranceway opened out into a large seating area. The pool table seemed to be the only change. Lounge chairs, wall décor, ceiling fan; all were just the same as before. There were just three other people there, it was still early, it should get busier later.

A couple sat in one corner, ignoring everything but each other. He was American, around forty, she was a local Philippina girl, she looked about twenty-five. They were engrossed. Their relationship was either very new or very deep – Paul couldn't decide which, but probably the former. It reminded him of his own past, he fought the sadness.

Everybody liked the corners, sitting in the middle of the room was too exposed. In the other corner at the front, with a view out into the street, was a man, around Paul's age, or maybe a bit younger. He nursed a Coors, so he was probably American. Paul sat on the next table, not too close to seem intrusive, but near enough, hopefully, to strike up a conversation.

Two barmaids completed the scene, lost in giggles and chat. Sporting low cut tops and sexily short uniform dresses, they glanced over and saw that Paul was seated.

Shyly, the younger one came up, smiling, and with notepad in hand.

"What'll it be?" at least she'd learned the language.

She returned with an opened Coors and set it down. His eyes followed her back to the bar until she disappeared behind, he noticed the guy on the next table doing the same and caught his eye.

"The scenery's pretty good around here." The man smiled, "yeah, it's better than anything back home, I guess."

"Have you been here long?" said Paul, and followed up with "Mind if I join you?"

"Not at all; glad of the company. I'm waiting for a friend, but he ain't showed yet, and by the way, been here fifteen years, straight out of the service. Got my discharge and never returned home. The name's Larry." "Hi Larry, I'm Paul." They shook hands.

"I'm guessing you're a vet too?" Larry asked. "Yup, two tours, Afghanistan. Marines – ended up sergeant." Larry raised his eyes, impressed but said nothing.

"I need a place to stay tonight, any recommendations? I'll stay around for a few days." Larry nodded at the bar.

"This place is as good a place as any, it gets lively later, but not too noisy. There'll be some girls for hire coming in later, if you get what I mean, and I think they've got six rooms they let out. It's a small place, but comfortable. It's been quiet for a while now."

Paul smiled. It seemed like things had not changed too much around here. He excused himself and made his way to the bar.

"Hi there, d'you have a room please, and what's the rate? I may stay around for a while."

The youthful girl smiled and got the registration book out, leaving it open on the desk.

"Just a minute, I'll get the manager." She disappeared up the stairs. His eyes followed her. She really did have a cute ass. Paul didn't have to wait long. An older, but attractive girl came into view.

"Hi there, I'm Jinky"

The petite Philippina smiled as she descended the rickety stairs.

"Welcome to Angeles City. How many nights d'you need?"

She glanced at the guest book. Paul could see there were not a lot of entries.

"Does this include breakfast?"

"Yes, as long as you're happy with local style – eggs, rice, sausage. Fish, bacon – that sort of thing. I'll do you a special rate if you're staying for a week. Is two hundred and fifty pesos a night ok?"

"That'll be fine, Jinky. Let's say a week for now, it might be longer."

Paul looked at the rate card on the counter and noted she'd given him a substantial discount. He handed over his credit card.

"Me and my husband run this place since he retired" she said as she processed the payment.

"He's a U.S. veteran, I guess the same as you."

"Yes, that's right. Is it so obvious?" She laughed.

"Around here, if you're over fifty and white, you're ex U.S. military." He smiled back.

"When will I get the pleasure of meeting him?"

"Oh, he'll be down soon, he takes a nap in the afternoon. He comes down around nine when it gets lively." Paul nodded. "Oh. I expect I'll still be around then."

"Your room will be ready in an hour, I'll bring your key over," she said as she went back up the stairs.

As he returned to his table Larry said "You'll like Joe, he's a regular guy. Navy seal, but he doesn't brag about it."

"I like him already."

Cute Ass wandered past, cleaning the tables, getting ready for the customers that would come in an hour or two. Paul looked over at Larry.

"D'you think…" Larry cut him off.

"Not a chance, mate. That one's taken. Married a sailor a few months ago, just waiting for her visa."

"Lucky guy, but if he's not here…" Larry laughed.

"They're not all like that, mate. Many of them are, but not that one – she's a loyal one – the guy's lucky."

"Yes, he is."

They relaxed with another beer and watched Cute Ass clean the tables – she was easy on the eye.

Three beers later they could smell the dinner being prepared in the kitchen, it smelled good. There was a choice, Chicken adobo, or beef tapas. Paul chose the chicken – the local beef could be very tough. Larry ordered them a malt whisky, a friendly gesture, and a great way to end the meal.

The bar was filling up now, mostly locals and their girlfriends, a couple for girls looking for trade, but they didn't take Paul's fancy. He'd wait and see – he wasn't in a rush. There was no wife to go home to, he reminded himself, but he had a nice bed bought and paid for upstairs. He felt more and more that he didn't want to be alone in it that night.

Angeles City was working its magic. Paul was settling in and becoming more his old self, the bar girls were giving him the eye, and that made him feel good, although he would wait and see if anything better turned up before making his choice.

Joe Timmins made an imposing figure as he descended the stairs. Slightly overweight, but clean shaven, he'd just celebrated his seventieth birthday. He could easily pass for twenty years younger. He was still as nimble and strong as many men half his age. Joe would not stand for any trouble in his bar and was always ready to throw out a troublemaker or three. There was rarely any trouble, especially when he was in the bar, and he made a point of being there most of the time.

Joe was at the bottom of the stairs when he noticed Larry and Paul, and smiled – he knew Larry well. He grabbed a beer from the refrigerator and opened it as he went past the bar. Jinky was still at the counter - he slapped his wife's bottom playfully as he passed, and sat with the two men. "Good evening, Larry. Who's the stranger?" Joe extended his hand with a smile.

"Well, I'm not so much a stranger, more a returner. I lived here many years ago."

That was as far as Paul wanted to go by way of explanation.

"Well. You're very welcome here, especially a marine vet."

"How did you know?"

"Well, that you're military is obvious, but remember, everything you say here is likely to be overheard."

He glanced over at the girls behind the bar. Paul smiled, he didn't mind being talked about, it couldn't do any harm.

Over several beers Joe told them of his army career, a similar story to most vets. He'd been stationed here for a while, but he'd met his wife Jinky in Manila. They married five years ago and bought the hotel from the former politician owner; it was quite run down at that time. He paid well over the odds for it, but he liked it.

There were profits to be made that didn't go through the books. Drugs were readily available anywhere in the Philippines, but buying them could be dangerous. Joe's customers believed they were safer buying from him rather that the dubious street sellers who would slit your throat if they could see a profit in it.

The inn was an enjoyable way of life. It kept his capable wife busy, and provided a good income. He enjoyed the trade and the lifestyle but missed his family in Ohio. Both his parents died long before he met Jinky, and he never heard from his ex-wife, but they had a son who had followed his father into military service. There was also a brother and sister still there. He returned back home as often as he could, but he didn't manage it every year.

Things had become more troublesome over recent months. Jinky was missing her family more, especially with her parents not being in the best of health. She would like to sell up and retire, but Joe was not ready for the quiet life yet, that is, he hadn't been until the local drug dealer showed interest in the business. Joe didn't like the arrogant young Chinese, but saying no to him may cause problems which he didn't need at his age.

***

Penny and Marsha breezed into the bar laughing. They were working girls. It was early for them, but it was worth checking if there might be any customers. Anyway, they lived close by and were short of cash.

As soon as they realized there were three white guys in the corner of the room, they were there like a shot. They knew Joe and Larry but there was an extra target tonight. "Hello ladies."

Joe offered them the two empty chairs at the table. Their short skirts rode up as they sat down.

"Can I get you girls a drink?" Paul broke the ice.

"Vodka and orange please." Penny said.

Cute Ass was already pouring the drinks.

"Excuse me a moment, ladies, I won't be long."

Paul hurried outside to fetch his overnight case from his car and headed upstairs. He wanted to check the room out, it looked as if he may have company tonight. The door was just on the left at the top of the stairs. Large windows made it bright, and it smelled fresh and clean. It was a good size. with a wide bed.

Everything was good, he was happy.

As he came out Jinky was there.

"Is everything ok?" she smiled.

"Yes, it's fine. It's a nice room." Paul made to go past her, but Jinky caught his arm.

"If you want my advice, take Marsha." Paul turned around, surprised.

"Penny gives a great blowjob, but Marsha will fuck all night and she has bigger boobs – they're not fake like mine."

She grabbed Paul's hand and put it down her dress, right over her right boob. His fingers grazed her nipple, it was quite large.

"Go on, have a feel – they cost Joe $5,000 – do you think it was worth it? Anyway, take Marsha – you won't regret it."

Paul just stood there, with his hand holding Jinky's breast. He looked over his shoulder, checking whether Joe was interested in what was happening.

"It's okay; Joe won't mind."

He smiled and gently removed his hand. Jinky just winked at him and walked off.

Paul came downstairs, wondering what had just happened. As he rejoined the table, Penny and Marsha were on their third drink and were feeling no pain, they'd both stopped trying to pull the hem of their short dresses down, they didn't care now.

Penny caught Paul looking as her dress rode up yet again.

"Do you like what you're looking at?"

She laughed, lifting the hem even higher and revealing the tiniest of red thongs."

"Wait a minute, Pen, let's give the man a choice."

Marsha lifted her skirt just a little, but it was enough to show she had no underwear at all and was shaved. Paul raised his eyebrows. Larry had drunk more than usual and was dozing in the corner, oblivious to what was going on.

In the company of the two other military vets, Joe too had taken more alcohol than he usually did, but he could hold his liquor and was up for a party. He leaned over and whispered.

"I hope you're not easily shocked, Paul."

"Far from it, Joe. Remember, I've been here before – I lived in Angeles about fourteen years ago."

Joe nodded and smiled.

"Go on girls, give the man a demo."

Penny moved closer to Joe; she didn't need further encouragement. She leaned over and rubbed him between his legs, which he obligingly opened. She got to work now. It took just two seconds for her to undo him. The young girl was oblivious to Joe's wife, Jinky, watching from the bar. She was laughing at the spectacle with the others; obviously they had a certain 'lifestyle' here, thought Paul.

Penny was hard at work now bobbing her head, with her mouth full. and her nearly bare ass in the air. Paul admired the scene and laughed with everyone else as Joe exploded into Penny's mouth. She wiped her lips with a napkin and looked over at the bar.

"How was that, Jinky?"

"Eight out of ten love, you brought him off too soon and didn't clean him up afterwards. Anyways, he'll last longer for me tonight if I can get him up again."

"Give me a shout if you have any trouble Jinky. I'll soon make him hard again." returned Penny.

The bar room banter and open sexual activity took Paul back to the old days. Angeles was the sex capitol of the Philippines at that time. It had not lost its charm. Paul smiled as Marsha leaned over and rested her hand on his knee.

"I'm just as good as her. If you take me upstairs, you won't regret it. And you don't have to use a condom, I'm safe now."

She purred into his ear and squeezed him before removing her hand. Paul remembered what Jinky had said.

"It's been a long day, I need to go up to bed now, Joe."

Joe smiled. Paul took Marsha's hand and she followed straight behind him. Larry had been drinking since lunchtime, he was still dead to the world.

It wasn't just the sex for Paul that night, it was the company. Marsha ended up staying over. They didn't sleep until two a.m., but Paul woke as usual at seven. Marsha did not stir when Paul pecked her on the cheek. It was so nice to sleep next to a girl again.

He could get used to her – he had to remind himself that she was just for rent and not for keeps. After watching her for a while he got up and made two coffees.

"Come on sleepy head, it's morning." He gently shook her shoulder. She smiled and got out of bed and sat at the small table, unashamed by her nakedness. Paul was grateful for the closeness and cuddles and well as for the sex, which was good. It was a long time since he had been so satisfied.

"Can you stay for breakfast?" he asked, without taking his eyes off her. "Of course, sweetie, as long as you like." She had an endearing smile.

Paul brought the two coffees over and sat down with her.

"There's no rush to get up, is there?" said Marsha, smiling.

She came towards him and kissed his lips as she pulled him free of the gown and towards the bed. She turned around and bent over the mattress.

Paul took the hint, and didn't need telling twice.

An hour later, they made their way down the creaky stairs. Joe was already having breakfast at his usual table. He looked up as they appeared.

"Did you have a good night? Actually, I don't have to ask – I can see from the look on your faces."

Joe stood to shake Paul's hand and the three sat down.

"You want an American breakfast, Paul? We have great sausage and bacon." "Sounds fine, thanks."

"I'll have the same," chirped in Marsha.

She hadn't let go of Paul's hand since they'd left the room. Joe nodded to the girls to bring over more pots of tea, and two more breakfasts. Joe poured Paul's tea for him.

"So, what brings you back to the City of Angels, Paul?"

"I was here during my service, Joe, and I've never lost my love for the place, and it's attractions."

Paul looked over at Marsha and smiled.

"I'm on my own now, so I was considering settling down now, there are worse places than Angeles, I suppose."

"Yes, there are," said Joe, he didn't ask why Paul was on his own. Years of experience had taught him not to ask too many questions. If a man wanted to tell you where he'd come from, geographically or emotionally, you wouldn't have to inquire.

Cute Ass was on duty again this morning. She came over to refill the coffees. Paul smiled at his thoughts, Cute Ass was the prettiest girl here, but the only one who didn't go with the customers, and that included Jinky, the wife of the owner.

"D'you want to go back upstairs?"

Marsha had finished her breakfast and hoped for more action and pay. Paul laughed.

"Come back in tonight. We'll see how it goes" Paul said.

He took 2,000 pesos from his wallet and handed it to her. She beamed.

"See you later then." She pecked him on the cheek and bounced out into the street.

The breakfast crowd was thinning out. A group of giggling bar girls occupied one corner, relaxing after a busy night, and two young businessmen huddled on a nearby table, in intense discussion. They looked Chinese, but Paul could not be sure. When Paul looked away the two men glanced around to make sure no one was watching before one of them produced a clear plastic envelope with white powder in it and passed it over quietly to the other who exchanged it for a small brown packet. Nobody saw, and they carried on about their business.

Paul rose, he planned to wander around the old neighbourhood and see what had changed. It was fifteen years since he was last here. He'd long ago lost contact with his old mates, but maybe some of them were still around. He felt better today and would be pleased to see some friendly faces. As he made to leave Joe caught his arm.

"Have you got a minute, Paul? There's something I'd like to chat with you about."

"Sure. I'm a man of leisure now, no place I have to be. What's on your mind?"

Joe moved a little closer and spoke quietly.

"I'm seventy now, Paul. I've been thinking it's time I gave this place up and took things easier, and Jinky wants to be closer to her family now they're getting older." Paul looked surprised.

"Are you offering me the hotel, Joe? I'd love to run a place like this, but I don't think I could afford it."

"Look, we've just met, but I believe in striking while the iron's hot. I do not want to miss an opportunity. The fact you're ex-marines is good enough for me. If you're interested, we can discuss the details later. I'm ok for cash, we can work out some sort of loan if you need it. I've made my money, and it's time I took things easier. You can't take it with you, mate. There are more important things in life than money."

Paul nodded; he was deep in thought.

"Well, if you're serious, let me consider it. I'll be here for a few days, so let's talk again later."

"Sure, but don't leave it too long. I've had other approaches, but not the right sort, if you know what I mean."

The old man looked around and moved Paul over to a quieter section where they could not be overheard.

"Take a good look at the accounts, Paul, but this hotel makes a lot more money than it shows on paper. You can take those figures and multiply them by ten with the other income streams."

Paul nodded; he wasn't sure what Joe meant but he had a good idea.

"You're a man of the world, Paul, and I believe you can take care of yourself, but if you're interested it's only fair that I tell you a couple of things."

The old man leaned back and ordered more coffees, then continued.

"The profit from the rooms, and the food and beverage, is good, and I'm basing the price on that only, but you can make many times that much with other products, I think you understand. I'll introduce you to my dealer, there won't be any problems."

Paul nodded, "You should also know that there is 'competition' in the city for the 'recreationals.' There's a group of Chinese gangsters here, Triads, who want to buy the place – I've put them off, and I don't think they'll be a big problem. I think they see that with all the U.S. ex-military men here, we'd be able to look after ourselves if we had to."

"Thanks for being upfront with me, Joe. That doesn't worry me, I've dealt with worse.

I'm sure you can imagine."

Joe had been discreet, and quiet, but he'd not noticed the young guys on the next table. They were speaking Chinese and he assumed they had no interest or understanding of the conversation going on next to them. He was wrong. They called for their bill and scurried out a few moments after Paul.

TWO

Hotel for Sale

Chinese immigrants were prominent in all the 'sin' businesses in the Philippines. Gambling, alcohol, tobacco, prostitutes, as well as money lending and hotels. The gangs kept a low profile, and generally kept the peace. The local police left them alone, partly because the gangsters often did their job for them, but in a more final way; but mostly because of the generous backhanders the Triads gave out.

Behind most of these enterprises was dirty Chinese money, triad money. Although they were based in China, Macao and Hong Kong, the triads had a growing influence in the more beautiful girl in Manila and had a son by her. Charles Wong (Charlie) had the same business mind as his father, and as the years passed by, he proved that he had the same cunning and ruthlessness as well. However, like many second-generation warlords, growing up in his father's shadow had protected him. He had an air of being able to do as he liked without fear of the consequences. Unlike his father who got things done mostly quietly, Charlie just did what he wanted when he wanted. His own family and workers feared him, and he increasingly became more unruly and difficult.

By the time Charlie was forty his father decided he should have his own patch and sent him to Angeles. Mainly to get him away from Manila where he was becoming a problem.

Angeles was a natural extension for 'the family,' and Charlie took it for a promotion, rather than the banishment which it truly was. It was full of girlie bars and cheap restaurants; everyone knew that Angeles was the place to go for the cheapest fuck in the Philippines.

There was money there, though. Some of the local girls snagged better off foreigners who made their home in Angeles or nearby Olongopo. Large U.S. army pensions funded the bars, the girls, and the growing drugs trade.

It was against this backdrop that Charlie arrived, with a bloodhound called Rex, and about twenty sturdy well-armed thugs.

At that time, the only casino in the town was owned by the mayor, Alonzo Vicente. He assumed the mayoralty from his father, a prominent local tradesman who proved himself good at politics and flourished before being stuck down with cancer. Alonzo was a disappointment to his father, who'd died the previous year. He was lazy, and although he's started with many healthy businesses, he was spending money faster than he could make it.

There were no children to pass anything on to, there was no wife. Alonzo was not the marrying kind.

Charlie's father, Xi, heard of the death of the old mayor, and of his hopeless only son, and decided now was the time to move in, so Charlie arrived.

He set up house and 'operations centre' in a substantial old building built by a U.S. army major who'd moved back home. Charlie bought it cheaply – with eight bedrooms and a few outbuildings it would do him, for now.

He wasted no time. His second day there he went to see Mayor Alonzo, with two of his minders – the biggest two.

The Mayor's office was a converted American social club. The walls were panelled in American style and the rooms large and well-decorated. The rambling old structure had a 'tired' feel – Alonzo had little time for maintenance.

"Does he know you're coming?"

The petite and businesslike girl with a big desk outside the Mayor's office had a feeling it would not matter whether he knew or not. They did not move. They were going to see the mayor.

"I'm sure he'll see us." Charlie forced a smile. It was his second day in the town, too soon to start hurting people, unless he had to. Rising carefully in the tight space, the secretary slid sideways and hugged the wall around to the double doors into the inner sanctum, she slipped in without knocking.

"There's a big guy here, sir – with two bigger guys. I think you need to see them."

Alonzo sighed. He'd heard the Wong family had come to town, but he'd not expected them so soon.

The Mayor was not an early riser and was generally regarded as lazy. There were papers piled all over the desk, and on the floor.

"Do they have guns?"

"If they do, I didn't see them." Alonzo looked over at his own 'protection.' An old guy asleep in the corner with a rusty rifle, he knew there were no bullets in it. He sighed.

"Okay, ask them to come in, please."

Before the girl could respond, the doors opened, and the three men strode in. Charlie approached the Mayor and held his hand out, smiling. There was no point doing this the hard way if you could do it the easy way.

"Hello Mr. Mayor. I'm Charlie, my father is Xi Wong, perhaps you've heard of him?"

"Oh yes, I have."

Alonzo rose and smiled as best he could and hoped that the bigger man would soon let go of his hand.

"Welcome to Angeles City, gentlemen. Please, take a seat." Alonzo smiled as he gestured to the chairs.

He gestured at the three upholstered chairs in front of his desk. Charlie sat, but the other men stood.

"Thank you, Mayor. It seems a pleasant city, congratulations on managing it so well. I think we'll be happy here." Alonzo smiled.

"Is there something I can do for you today, or is this just a courtesy visit?"

"Mayor Alonzo. We're gonna get along just fine here, and I think it's better if we're frank and upfront with each other from the start, don't you?"

The Mayor was still smiling.

"I need something to keep my boys busy."

He gestured at the men standing behind him.

"Otherwise they can get into mischief, and they can cause real trouble if they have time on their hands – do you get my meaning?"

The Mayor nodded, he understood completely what Charlie was trying to say.

"We checked out a couple of places last night. No point wasting any time is there? You've got a nice little place just down the street – the casino, I think it's called Paradise? Looked nice, but a little rundown – maybe it needs some investment? How much would you want for it?"

"It's not for sale Charlie. My dad started that – I want to continue it. Sorry, there's lots of other suitable places, perhaps I can recommend some businesses?" Charlie rose.

"Everyone has his price, Alonzo." He decided it was time to drop the 'Mr. Mayor.'

"I'm sure you'll see that it's the best thing to sell. My 'investors' are very keen and used to getting what they want. I'll give you some space to think. We'll call back tomorrow. Have a pleasant day."

The trio stood and left, before the mayor could reply. So, the triads, the Chinese mafia, had come to town. Alonzo stared at the portrait of his father on the wall and wondered if the old man had dealt with anything like this, and what he would do. On his way out of the Mayor's office he'd already decided his next course of action, and it would be soon.

Angeles City came to life around nine p.m. each night. The girlie bars, the restaurants, the hotels, and all entertainment places livened up, and most clubs would keep going through the small hours until the sun rose.

Weeknights tended to be quieter, so it was only just after one a.m. when the last punter fell out of the front door of Paradise casino and staggered homeward, drunk and a lot poorer than when he went in. The bright lights clicked off, darkening the street. Soon after that, the Casino manager, Dodie, locked the doors and, accompanied by a disinterested old guard with a dirty, rusting weapon, made off towards the Mayor's house with the night's takings, just short of a million pesos, it was still a good night for a Tuesday.

Dodie turned sixteen a few summers ago. He was a popular lad and held his birthday party in the local bar owned by his dad; it was well attended. Alonzo, the mayor's son, was a little older. He insisted on buying the boy a drink to celebrate his birthday, and then another.

The young man went home with Alonzo that night. The last thing he remembered was being naked in bed with Alonzo. He stayed with Alonzo after that and jumped at the chance to run the Casino when Alonzo's father died, and the old manager retired. He was good with figures, and everyone knew about his relationship with the boss, so despite his youth, it surprised no one.

The dusty streets were quiet; few people were around at this time of night. Those that were could hardly walk straight. Dodie put the takings into the usual blue canvas bag, and into his rucksack. He turned the key in both large locks which protected the front door until he heard them click.

Every night's routine was the same. The 'guard' followed him down the street. Tonight was the same as any other night, until suddenly it wasn't.

Three masked men came out of nowhere. The old man raised his gun. Before he could lift it above his waist, he lost consciousness as the closest man confronted him. The powerful uppercut to the jaw floored him and knocked him out. His assailant followed through, kicking him in the ribs; he groaned. One of the others pulled the attacker away from the gasping old man.

"That's enough, no more. You know what the boss said. Don't hurt them too much."

The thug backed away. The old man was awake now, with pains in his face and his stomach, but he thought better of trying to move, and played dead.

Dodie gripped the money bag tightly and regarded his protector lying prone on the floor, and the three large men coming towards him. Things did not look good; he had to think quickly.

"Take it." Hs said, as he thrust the bag at chest of the nearest man.

"You can have it all. Just don't hurt me."

Dodie pushed it into the man's chest. He let it fall to the ground.

"If only life were that simple, son." said the man.

You could see his grin through his face covering "We don't want your money." The big man turned to the other two.

"Come on, let's get this over with."

Tony, the leader of the trio, was Charlie's most trusted aide; he'd been with him for many years. There was nothing he would not do for his boss.

The three men hustled Dodie down a small alley; it was very narrow and blocked at the end. Tony pushed him forward while the other two took up their positions at the top of the entrance. No one else would go down that alley, at least for the next ten minutes. Smiling at the frightened youth, Tony unbuckled his pants. When Tony was done, they left the youth half naked on the ground and strolled off back towards the casino.

Luckily for Dodie, they were close to the Mayor's house. For a while he lay sobbing, his pants still round his ankles. The men had long gone and no-one else was around as he dragged himself out of the alley and towards home and safety.

Just beyond the alley, the old man still lay sprawled in the gutter. The few people who passed him just assumed he was drunk. Dodie saw him in the road and ran over to him.

"Stay there, friend, don't move. I'll get help."

Dodie knelt down and touched the old man's shoulder, he grunted.

Dodie still had the money, but he was sore, walking was difficult. His assailant worked quickly, no lubricant and no care. Two thrusts and he was deep inside – Dodie winced at the memory, and the pain.

"What happened to you, are you all right, have you been robbed?"

The guard on the gate saw him struggling along the road and came out to help. Taking his shoulder, he guided the limping Dodie into the safety of the Mayor's courtyard.

"No. The money's all there, they took nothing." *Nothing you can count,* thought Dodie.

"Get some men, they hurt my guard, he's by the alley close to the casino. Hurry, man – get him to hospital. Don't worry, I'm ok. I can see to myself now. It's better if you say nothing about this. I'll explain to the Mayor."

Even in agony, Dodie couldn't sleep without a shower. He washed himself; there was just a little blood now. For no good reason, Dodie was ashamed and hoped no one else would find out, except, of course, for Alonzo; he had to know. He'd face Alonzo in the morning, at least he'd not lost the money, but they'd given him a stark warning to pass to the Mayor.

Breakfast would be in about three hours. Dodie didn't want to sleep. He lay on his bed, he couldn't sit down, and waited until seven.

At exactly seven he walked straight into Alonzo's bedroom and ran up and hugged his still sleeping lover, he couldn't hold back the tears. As they had ordered him, he recounted the entire episode, in detail. Alonzo said nothing, but stared into space.

The Wong family were successful for two reasons. They knew what they wanted, and how to get it. They rarely failed in either respect. As far as Alonzo could see they'd already won. His lover was laying upstairs, violated, as a warning to co-operate with the Triads. The local police chief and his own security had no appetite for a confrontation with the Wongs. They'd both urged him to settle with Charlie at any price to avoid any more trouble.

Charlie had more men than him and could ask his dad for more. Alonzo could not even rely on the local police – they were frightened of the triads. Charlie knew how to hurt the Mayor, and it wasn't through his wallet. Unlike his dad, Alonzo was a coward. Charlie had banked on that.

The guard didn't keep quiet of course, and by lunchtime everyone knew there'd been an 'incident.' Alonzo cancelled his meetings for the day and hid in his office, refusing any visitor, except a chosen few. For two hours he'd met with his chief of police and his own head of security. During the meeting they learned that the old man who was supposed to guard the boy and the money did not survive. The kick in the stomach ruptured his already damaged liver. He died at the hospital an hour ago.

***

The three burly men met no opposition as they entered the building and made straight for the Mayor's office.

"Don't worry I don't need an appointment." Charlie brushed past the gaping girl and swept into the Mayor's office.

"Hello Alonzo, nice to see you again. How are you today?"

Alonzo looked up surprised, and now frightened

"What do you want Charlie? I thought I made my position clear yesterday."

He tried to make a show and sound confident, but a quavering voice gave him away. Charlie laughed.

"Oh yes, you did. Loud and clear. But I thought you may have had a change of mind. I hear you're even having trouble protecting your closest 'friends'"

The emphasis was noted.

"These are tough times. Let me take some of the strain off you."

Alonzo seethed inside but there was nothing he could do.

"How much are you offering?"

He was asking just for the sake of saying something, he knew he would take whatever the powerful warlord offered.

"Well, I think the value's going down. It seems we will need to pay for more security, we'll want to keep our people safe at night."

Charlie reached into his coat pocket and threw a piece of paper on the desk. It was a simple sale agreement. Alonzo noticed it bore the details of the biggest law firm in town. *So, Charlie had them in his pocket as well*, he thought.

Alonzo glanced down at the paper, and then up at the towering man.

"You know that's much less than it's worth, don't you?'

"Well, my friend, it's only worth what someone will pay for it, and I don't think, under the circumstances, there would be any other buyers do you?"

Charlie walked behind the desk and put his arm around the despairing man. Alonzo flinched, but was too scared to pull away.

"Come on Alonzo, sign the paper, you can't avoid it. Could you live with yourself if there were any more 'incidents'? I think you'll find that if you wait, the price will be even lower,'"

Alonzo signed, there was nothing else he could do. From that moment he no longer owned the casino.

"That's better Mayor, I told you yesterday we'd get along just fine. I'll send someone round with the money tomorrow, and we don't need any of your staff, we'll find our own. You can tell your manager that he can rest now, I'm sure he needs time for his... pride... to stop hurting."

Charlie's thugs sniggered.

If Alonzo had been a stronger man that would have been a breaking point, but Charlie always had the measure of the men he dealt with. He knew he wouldn't have any trouble with the spineless politician.

***

That was over five years ago. By the time Paul returned to the town, Charlie and his gang had their feet well under the table. Along the way, they'd built a second casino, so they owned the only two casinos in town, and no-one else could open one – the Mayor would not issue any more licenses.

They added three bars and a wholesale liquor business – so no-one could sell beer or spirits in the town now without their blessings. The gang also owned a large bakery on the outskirts of town where they stored the drugs and other smuggled goods brought over from Hong Kong or mainland China. A sizeable share of the massive profits found its way to the family in Manila, and on to the Triads in Hong Kong. That was common knowledge. They brought their tremendous resources to bear on anyone who objected to anything they did, and made a few choices examples of those who crossed them; most of them ended up in the local graveyard, so for the last few years, they'd sewn up and run the town with little dissent or opposition.

Charlie continued to be a disappointment to his father. His excessive drinking and temper made him an unpredictable partner. Every time he returned to Manila, he had raging arguments with the old man. His visits became less frequent and, after she didn't see him for two years his long-suffering wife gave up the fight. She stopped bothering him; he was fine with that. Divorce did not exist in the Philippines, and annulment was out of the question unless Charlie wanted it, and he didn't.

Now, the group had their sights on the Blue Room Hotel. It was just off Walking street in the Balibago district, Charlie had a good view of the imposing building from his office window, and it annoyed him that he didn't own it.

He'd approached Joe about selling, the old man had asked for time to consider it. Joe was no fool, he was aware that outright refusal might bring reprisals. But Charlie was no fool either. You didn't mess with U.S. veterans. There would be many skilled and fearless vets living locally who would come to his aid. Charlie would win, but it would be a costly battle.

Charlie sat with his mid-morning coffee in the storeroom at the casino. Two of his junior men stood before him, frightened.

"What do you mean? He's selling the place to someone else? He wouldn't dare. The old fool knows what I can do to him."

Crimson with rage, the Triad boss paced the floor like a caged animal. He threw his coffee cup at the helpless messengers, the two men who'd been having breakfast there that morning and overheard Joe's conversation with Paul.

The closest guy ducked the cup, but it hit the smaller man in the head leaving a slight cut.

"Say nothing to anyone about this, understand." The men scampered for the door, but Charlie stopped them.

"Wait. Did you say that Paul said he'd talk to Joe later?"

The men nodded, eager to please.

"Make sure you take your meals there now and stay there in the evenings. I want to be told the minute those two men say as much as 'Good Morning' to each other, is that understood?"

They nodded again.

"Okay, now get out and do your job. Do not fail me. And send me up another coffee," he shouted after the departing pair.

Everyone knew what happened if you failed the boss, they would make sure they did not.

No one would question them taking their meals at the hotel, they were often there anyway. They usually occupied the same small table with two chairs, conveniently within earshot of the corner table where Joe, and sometimes his wife, took their breakfasts.

The next day, Paul came down to breakfast at the same time as usual, on his own. Perhaps he hadn't taken a girl last night. Charlies men sat already in place in the far corner sipping beer. They noted him coming down on his own.

"Perhaps he's too old to do it every day now. Perhaps he can only get it up once a week."

The pair sniggered to themselves as their breakfast arrived.

Paul ate breakfast alone and left soon after nine o'clock. Joe had not come down for breakfast that morning. Neither of them appeared for lunch, and in the evening, Joe sat in the usual corner, but there was no sign of Paul.

The following day Charlie's men struck lucky. Paul came down again, alone, but this time Joe was there and rose to meet him as he approached.

"Good morning, Paul. You're looking well today."

The old man gestured to the empty chair on the other side of the table, Paul sat down.

"Good morning Joe, great to see you again, I was hoping to find you here." They made themselves comfortable as coffee arrived.

"I've been looking around Angeles, there are a lot of changes since I was last here – and all for the better. I feel at home." Paul looked around at the decor.

"Does that mean you're interested in my little proposition?"

Charlie's men were on the next table, trying hard not to seem interested in the conversation next to them, and no-one took any notice of them, anyway.

"Possibly, at the right price. Do you have any accounts? I'd like to see the figures before I decide."

"Of course, not a problem."

He pulled an envelope from his jacket pocket.

"Here's the profits for the last six months, and a balance sheet and stock list. I prepared these yesterday – I hoped you'd be interested. I'm not looking for a big lump sum. I've drawn up a little repayment schedule – take a look."

Paul put the papers into the briefcase he carried with him.

"Thanks Joe. Give me a day or two to consider things; I won't keep you waiting.

"This isn't a sudden decision. I've thought about it a lot, Paul. Money is not an issue. I'm not out to screw anyone – I don't need to."

The next two mornings Joe made a point of being down for breakfast early, but Paul did not appear. On the third morning,

Paul sat downstairs nursing his first coffee before Joe arrived. He smiled as Joe came over.

"Good morning Joe, I've kept your seat warm."

He moved to let Joe sit in his usual chair.

Neither man was big on small talk.

"Is there anything you want to know? Have you made your mind up yet?" Joe looked quizzically at the younger man.

"Oh yes, we have a deal. I'm looking forward to running the hotel, and the money is fine. It will be in place in a few days. I'll be able to do it all in one go, but thanks for the finance offer."

"Well that's great," said Joe, trying to not look relieved. "Jinky will be pleased. We'll only take our personal stuff; we'll leave everything else here."

"Well. That's fine by me. I'll check things out with my lawyer and my bank, perhaps you can get some papers drawn up."

"How soon do you want this to happen, Paul?"

"Well, it's the 24th of the month now – let's aim for the 31st – clean start for a new month is that ok?"

"It sure is. I'll get working on the papers I'll let you know if there are any issues."

"Likewise."

Charlie's men waited until Paul and Joe left, then paid their bill. They couldn't wait to tell their boss the news. They were nervous about telling their boss the news. He was very likely to shoot the messenger.

It was mid-morning, Charlie's quiet time. He liked to take his morning coffee in peace. He was not happy when his hapless spies rushed into the room.

"This better be good, boys. I don't like to be disturbed during my break."

"Sorry, boss, but we've got some news about the hotel. The old guy did a deal with an American, I believe he is a vet – he acted like one. They shook on it and everything."

"No, it can't be. You must have misheard. The old fool wouldn't dare cross me. He told me he'd think about my offer. He knows who I am, he wouldn't go behind my back."

"Perhaps he was trying to do the deal without you knowing, boss. He didn't realize we heard the conversation."

"He'll regret it. I'll make sure of that, and I'll still end up with the hotel."

Charlie thought for a moment.

"Joe has a pretty young wife?"

He looked at the other for confirmation, they nodded.

"I'll bet she'd sell to me; she wouldn't want any trouble."

"D'you want us to kill him, boss? He's old and overweight, we could wait 'till they closed up, and sneak in."

"Too risky, someone might see, and I bet he keeps a gun close, and don't forget he's an army vet – even the old ones can be dangerous.

We need to be careful. Find out some more about the old man. Where he goes, what he does, that sort of thing, and get back to me as soon as you can. Now get out. Make sure you're always at the hotel. I want to hear if they say anything else to each other."

When the men had left, Charlie phoned his dad.

"Hello dad. How are you?"

"What's up son. You only ever call me when you want something."

Charlie bristled, but didn't say anything because his dad was right.

"Sorry, dad, but we're busy here. I'm trying to buy the Blue Room hotel – I've mentioned it to you before."

"Yes, I remember, son. The owner didn't want to sell, and he's a foreigner. I told you to be cautious. Why is it so important to you to get the place?"

"We don't own any hotels here, dad. It would be very useful, but there's another reason. It looks like a small, upmarket hotel – I'm sure that part makes a tidy profit, and there's more to it than that. Its clientele is mainly ex-pats, U.S. military. This is the place they buy their drugs – it's well known, and the stuff they get doesn't come from us. It's run by another group, we need that hotel to consolidate our business, and our profits. Joe takes a cut, I've tried to get our product in there, but he won't have it. I can't get too hard – most of the clients are foreigners, they're not as easy to deal with as locals."

His father understood the issues, but was wary of tackling foreigners, especially military vets. Charlie was used to getting his own way, he was not skilled in negotiation. Xi was not sure his son could deal with a situation like this, but he had to let him try.

"Well, do what you have to, son. But please be careful, put some pressure on the owner, but carefully."

"Okay, dad. I'll do what needs to be done."

He puts the phone down without saying goodbye, their calls usually ended like that.

Charlie strode out into the Casino. Tony was supervising the cleaning as his boss approached.

"I've got another job for you, Tony."

***

Wild boar still roamed the hills around Angeles City. For many years it had been illegal to hunt them, but people flouted the law; the local police ate well in return for turning a blind eye. The juicy pigs appeared on restaurant menus and butchers displays everywhere. This was the Philippines.

The hotel ran itself these days, all Joe did was to bank the money and pay the bills. Occasionally he had to deal with any customers who'd had too much to drink, but this became less and less of a problem as his reputation for no nonsense spread.

Fishing and hunting were his passions. Every month he would go out into the bay with a local fishing boat and his two sturdy rods. Once he brought back a swordfish, but it was usually yellow fin tuna, or sea bass.

He also hunted about once a month. The mountains around Angeles were covered with thick jungle and forests which were teeming with tasty things to eat. He would always come home with something. A deer, or perhaps some rabbits. Sometimes, if you were lucky, you could bag a wild boar or two.

He and his friends would set off early in the morning so they could get deep into the forest before the sun got too hot. They would often kill one or two, animals at least. He would later serve his share in the restaurant.

He was in an excellent mood today. He'd done a deal with Paul and could soon relax. It would be a pleasant day for hunting. His friends couldn't come, so it would be just him and his local guide and helper, Maxwell.

The old man befriended the young Philippino soon after he bought the hotel.

Maxwell drank regularly there, but seemed more responsible than many of his friends. He worked for the Mayor as a handyman and did odd jobs for Joe.

Joe paid him well for the hunting trips and gave him a share of the meat as well. Joe found out that Maxwell had a young family and struggled financially.

Excitedly, he packed some sandwiches and a few beers. The sun just rose, and Jinky was not up yet. Cute Ass had started work and was cleaning the bar when Joe left.

"When she gets up can you tell Jinky I've gone hunting. I'm picking Maxwell up on the way. It's only the two of us today – I only decided last night and no one else is free."

"Sure, Joe, I'll tell her. Good luck. I hope you get something."

Cute Ass watched out the window to see Joe's station wagon pull away before she pulled out her phone. She answered it straight away.

"I have something to tell you...'

The person at the other end listened without saying a word.

'*This is my chance*' Thought Charlie.

When Joe pulled up at Maxwell's house, it was not Maxwell that greeted him, but another man who let him in. Joe didn't recognize him. Maxwell came through from the kitchen.

"Joe. This is my cousin Alexander. Do you mind if he comes with us? He's staying with me for a visit."

Alexander nodded and smiled. He seemed older than Maxwell, and bigger. Joe wondered if he'd ever been a boxer. He shook hands with the tall man.

"No, that will be fine. Jump in."

Joe moved his bag over in the back seat to make room for the Alexander. A few miles out of Angeles the jeep left the dirt road and plowed through overgrown tracks through the undergrowth into denser jungle.

He'd visited a couple of the other hotels; he wanted to check out the competition.

Joe climbed steadily up the mountain.

Five miles away, Paul got back to the Hotel. It was around mid-morning. He'd visited a couple of the other hotels; he wanted to check out the competition. Cute Ass was cleaning the tables and Jinky checked the cash behind the bar. She looked up and smiled as he appeared.

"Hi Paul, that's good timing – have coffee with me, Joe's gone hunting. I could do with the company."

"Sure," said Paul sitting down in his usual place.

"I always take coffee in my room, come on up."

Cute Ass sniggered as Paul followed Jinky up the stairs. Paul wouldn't be wanting another girl tonight.

Jinky's chambers were very feminine – lots of drapes, pastel curtains, and scatter cushions, and a small circular table with two chairs in the corner beside the door to the bedroom.

As they chatted, the cook brought in coffee, and fresh cookies.

"Make yourself at home, I'll just get changed."

Jinky disappeared into an adjoining room - she emerged five minutes later in the briefest of gowns.

"I didn't think you'd mind the informality, Paul, anyway, you've met these two before." Giggling, she opened the gown to reveal her breasts, then sat down at the table leaving her clothes open.

A few miles away, the sun was rising in the sky as Joe and his party wound around the hill, making their way up the steep slopes towards the denser tropical jungle. When they neared the top, the vegetation became too dense for their vehicle. They left the jeep behind and trudged into the undergrowth. Alexander and Joe followed silently in the footsteps of Maxwell – he' learned where the boars were likely to be.

Back at the hotel, Paul was enjoying his coffee

"Are you enjoying the view?" Jinky asked playfully, wiggling her breasts as Paul sipped his coffee.

"You have magnificent boobs, Jinky. Joe is very lucky."

"Not just Joe. Love. We have what I think people call an 'open marriage.' We both like it that way."

Jinky winked at Paul, letting the gown slip from her shoulders

She rose and Paul saw that she was naked. Without a word she pulled him by the hand out of his seat and towards the bedroom. *Oh, well, sex before lunchtime, another novel experience*, thought Paul.

Back in the forest, Maxwell signaled for the group to stop. Listening intently, his hand in the air, he pointed in front and to his right.

"Over there, in the bushes, I think I can see a boar, in fact there's a family of three," whispered Maxwell, pointing to a thicket about thirty yards away.

"Get ready, they will come into view anytime soon."

Joe stepped forward and kneeled down, resting his rifle on a log. His eyes were fixed on the bush ahead, scouring the foliage for movement. He checked his sights and waited for his prey to appear. Alexander lagged behind, but Maxwell quietly gave him a nod. From inside his coat Alexander produced a sturdy hunting knife. Stealthily, he crept towards Joe from behind.

The old man was concentrating on the thought of killing a boar. He paid no heed to the noises as Alexander slowly crept forward.

In the hotel, coffee was over. Paul was being undressed, and he did not object at all. Jinky pulled down his pants and shorts and admired his physique.

"Ha, I thought you'd be big." Jinky laughed.

She led him to the bed. She was holding him. He was ready.

She was already wet and sighed as Paul entered her. Paul lunged now with an increasing rhythm. Jinky grunted with each push.

In the Jungle, Alexander was above the prone man. His right arm came down swiftly and forcefully. His knife entered Joe's back.

"Argh." Joe groaned. The sharp knife worked expertly between his ribs and nicked his heart just enough to cause it to burst. Arterial blood spurted out under pressure as he fell to the ground groaning.

The old man's heart gave up the effort to beat just as, back at the hotel, Paul emptied himself into the now dead man's wife.

Alexander drove Joe's car back down the hill, he dropped Maxwell off before the main road and headed back into the forest. He would leave the car deep enough inside that it was unlikely to be found soon, if ever.

***

Paul was later to breakfast the next morning, it was past ten o'clock when he descended the stairs into the dining area. There was no one else there, which was unusual, it rarely emptied until past eleven. He noted that the two young Chinese guys who usually had their breakfast in the hotel had not appeared today. As he waited for his bacon and eggs he reflected on the day before. He'd finally made it to his own room midafternoon. One session was not enough for Jinky.

He was proud of himself this morning – two times. It'd been a long time since he'd managed that, and she was good. She let him know she was available anytime. Joe wouldn't mind. Her husband had his own interests; the arrangement worked very well for both of them.

Jinky came down the stairs not long after, but she didn't return Paul's smile. She hurried over to him and sat down close to him. Her face was fraught and pale. She had not made up as she usually did before appearing.

"Joe didn't come home last night, Paul. I'm very worried."

"Perhaps he stayed with someone else?" said Paul.

Jinky shook her head.

"He wouldn't do that. Joe always told me where he was going. He was supposed to be hunting yesterday – I've tried to call his friend Maxwell, they always go together, but he's not answering."

"Maybe they had an accident, I'll go up into the woods and take a look if you like."

"Oh, please Paul, can you? The local police won't take any notice unless I pay them lots of money – and even then, I can't rely on them."

Just then, Jinky's phone rang. It was Maxwell.

"Good morning Jinky, how are you?"

"I'm fine, Maxwell. Is Joe with you?"

"No, I was expecting him yesterday for hunting, but he never showed up. Isn't he with you?"

Jinky gasped, the blood drained from her face.

"He was supposed to be going hunting with you, but he didn't come home. Do you have any idea where he might be? I'm worried, he's never done this before."

"It's too early to worry, Jinky. I'm sure he met some friends, or maybe a girl. He probably got drunk and he's sleeping it off somewhere. He'll be alright, I'm sure. Try not to worry. Let me know when he shows up."

Maxwell put the phone down. There were tears in his eyes. He turned on Alexander, the man standing behind him; Maxwell was angry.

"Why did you have to kill him? You said you just wanted to frighten him. He was a nice old man – he didn't deserve that."

Alexander stared at him, his knife, now cleaned, visible in his belt.

Tony came through from the kitchen and rested an arm on Maxwell's shoulder.

"He upset the boss, Max, you can't upset the boss and get away with it. He sent me around to see you this morning to make sure you'd keep your mouth shut. I told him you wouldn't say anything about it. You know what the boss can do. He wouldn't think twice about hurting your family. Please tell me we don't have to worry about you."

"Yeah, you've already told me. I won't say a word, I just wish I hadn't been there. Why did you have to involve me?"

"Joe trusted you and would happily go into the forest with you. Don't worry, no-one will know you helped us."

"I hope not. I'm only thinking about my family."

"Here, dry your tears with these, Tony put ten US$100 bills on the table. Maxwell looked at them and only picked them up and quickly slipped them into his pocket when his wife, Marites, came into the kitchen.

"You boys want some coffee?" Tony declined and said his goodbyes, giving Maxwell a long hard stare as he left.

***

Back at the hotel, things were happening. Cute Ass rushed through to the dining room.

"Ma'am Jinky, come quick, it's the police."

Jinky was helping to clear up after the breakfast service, it took her a few seconds to understand what Cute Ass was saying. She shook herself.

"I'll be right there."

Officer Rodriguez sat in the corner waiting. He was not in a rush; Cute Ass gave him a coffee. He wasn't sure how to convey the news. This was the first time he'd had to advise the next of kin of the death of a loved one. Jinky bustled in.

"Hello officer, how are you? It's a pleasure to see you. What can we do for you?"

She tried to smile, but inside her stomach was knotted and she felt sick. This could not be good news.

"Is your husband here?" enquired the young policeman.

He was treading cautiously; they weren't yet certain that the disfigured body they found yesterday was Joe.

"No. He's been gone since yesterday morning. He should have come home last night, I've been worried. Is this about Joe? Is he okay?"

"Jinky, I am so sorry to have to tell you, but I think we've found Joe, up the hill in the forest. He's dead I'm afraid."

Although part of Jinky expected news of this sort, to hear it was like a punch in the gut, she sat down opposite to the officer.

"What do you mean 'you think'? What don't you know? Is there a chance it isn't Joe?"

Rodriguez looked uncomfortable now, but he had no choice but to carry on.

"It looks like some sort of accident. Those big boars can be vicious, I'm afraid we only knew it was him from his wallet, his body is badly... damaged."

"What do you mean damaged?"

"We had an anonymous phone call saying there was a body there. There was some sort of accident."

He didn't have the heart to tell the pretty widow that the wild boars and other animals had already consumed a lot of the flesh before the police reached him."

The policeman leaned over and held Jinky's hand now. Her head was in her hands she was convulsing with tears.

"He should never have gone up there alone; it's dangerous to hunt wild pigs, you need at least two or three of you." Jinky was bewildered.

"He was supposed to go with Maxwell, but Maxwell said Joe never went there."

"Well how did he get there then, there's no sign of a car? We thought maybe you took him up there and left him."

"No, I didn't. I wouldn't. I know better than that. How did he die? Did someone kill him?

He doesn't have any enemies – everyone liked him."

"We can't be sure, the body is pretty messed up, I'll ask the boss if we can let the pathologist take a look and let you know, but it's likely he just tripped and the pigs got him. It looks like he was on his own."

Jinky just stared at the man. Something wasn't right. Joe was a seasoned hunter; he would never be up there on his own.

THREE

The Funeral

Paul was unaware of the visit; he was just getting up when the police officer called. He showered and changed quickly. After breakfast, he would go up into the hills looking for Joe. His shirt was half on when he heard the quiet knock at the door.

"Can you come down, sir? Ma'am Jinky wants to see you, she's very upset." Cute Ass stood there expectantly; Paul could see she had been crying.

"Oh, why is she upset, and why are you upset? What's happened?"

"It's better you come down; she needs you."

Without waiting for a response, the serving girl hurried back down the stairs. Paul finished dressing and made his way to the bar. Jinky stood alone behind the bar, her eyes red and puffy, staring at the wall.

"Oh, Paul. He's dead. They just found his body."

Paul did not need to ask who. He came closer and put a comforting arm around her shaking shoulders. She rested her head on his chest and they just stayed that way for a while. Jinky would talk when she was ready. Finally, after some sweet tea, she was calmer.

"What shall I do Paul, can you help me? I just don't know what I should do."

Slowly and carefully she explained what the policeman said, and then went quiet. Paul guided her to the nearest chair.

"Don't worry Jinky, I'll take care of everything that has to be done; you go and lie down. There's nothing for you to do now. I'll see you tonight. We'll discuss things over dinner, if you're up to it. Go and rest, love. You don't have to be down here today."

Paul nodded at Cute Ass who was watching from the counter. She came over and helped her boss up the stairs.

Paul ate little of his breakfast. Something was wrong here. How could Joe have got there? Someone took him up, and if not Maxwell, who? And why would Joe lie about going with Maxwell? Perhaps he just had a change of plan.

Paul's concern now was for Jinky, she needed his help. He'd go to the police station himself tomorrow, he hoped they'd let him see the body, then a visit to Maxwell, then the undertaker – he'd take as much strain off Jinky as he could.

Jinky sneaked quietly downstairs just before the dinner service started. She looked like a ghost as she descended the stairs, but that was an improvement on a few hours ago. Paul sat in his usual place nursing a beer. There was a somber atmosphere in the hotel today. As soon as he spotted her, Paul stood, taking her arm, and guided her into the chair next to him.

She didn't look at Paul, she just stared absently through the window.

"What's my future now, Paul?"

Her face was ashen. Her world had been taken away abruptly, she was numb and frightened.

"When Joe told me you would buy the place, I was so pleased. That would have suited Joe and me – we could have gone off to America knowing the business was in safe hands."

Paul just listened as she continued.

"Before you came along, I thought he would have to sell out to Charlie. I was dreading it. All the staff were. I was so glad he didn't.

Charlie's an evil man." It puzzled Paul.

"Who is this Charlie? Why didn't you want Joe to sell to him?"

Jinky's face became dark and drawn.

"Charlie and his gang have been the ruin of this town. He and his triad thugs came here from Manila a few years ago and took over the city. Anyone who got in their way always regretted it, if they lived."

"Joe mentioned something about them. I've come across guys like that before, Jinky. People must stand up to criminals like that. I'm sure I can get some lads together. We'll sort them out." Paul smiled.

"No, it's much worse than that. Charlie is a dangerous man. His father is a Godfather in Manila. He controls the gambling, drugs, alcohol, and other 'businesses' in Tondo and Manila –

They're part of the triad society from China – they have so much power nobody can stand up to them. They've paid off the politicians, the police, everybody in authority. They can do that they want now."

"Why are they interested in a small place like Angeles?"

"Appearances are deceptive, Paul. Angeles may be small, but because of the US forces that used to be here, there's a lot of money flowing through the girlie bars and hotels. When Charlie came, he forced the local Mayor to sell the town's only casino to him. Since then no-one will stand up to them. They have another casino now, and a few hotels – and they want this one. Perhaps I'll have to sell to them."

"Don't be too hasty, Jinky. I'm still interested in buying, but let's get over the next few days first. I'll talk to the police first thing tomorrow to see if they've got an autopsy report yet, and I'll see the funeral director for you."

He also intended to pay a call on Maxwell, but he didn't tell Jinky this.

"There's no need for you to worry, I'll do what's necessary, try to rest."

"Oh, Paul, I'm so glad you're here. I don't know how I would cope on my own."

"Well, you're not on your own, love, I'm not going anywhere."

He gave her a hug, then helped her up the stairs. Paul did not sleep well that night. There was something very fishy about this business. He resolved to get to the bottom of it.

***

Paul rose early the next morning. As expected, Jinky did not appear for breakfast. The atmosphere in the hotel was quiet, the staff were still shocked, and did not know what would happen now. Were their jobs safe?

Paul made his way through the dusty streets to the police station. It was still in the same place. As he turned the corner, he noticed they had redecorated it since his time there. It had seen better days. The once imposing building needed repair. Paint flaked off the once imposing concrete columns. The old rust red paint was now gray, and it had an illuminated sign above the entrance – 'Police.'

Built many years ago while thousands of American troops billeted in the town, it was really too large now. More officers were needed at that time.

Only thirty officers now rattled around in a building made for more than a hundred men.

The inside was large, but seemed gloomy and clinical, a few people milled around. It looked untidy. An older sergeant stood behind the counter looking busy with papers. The expansive entrance lobby was otherwise deserted and the battered wooden reception desk had seen better days.

"Can I speak with officer Rodriguez, please?"

Jinky had given him the name of the officer who'd given her the news. The sergeant nodded and indicated a row of chairs against the far wall.

"Take a seat. I'll check if he's here."

After ten minutes a fresh-faced, smartly dressed young officer appeared. He approached Paul and shook his hand.

"Are you Paul?" He smiled and held his hand out. "Jinky mentioned you when I visited her. I'm glad you're there for her, she will need some help for a while."

He was younger than Paul imagined, but seemed friendly and efficient.

"I'll do the best I can. She asked me to call in to ask if you've come up with a cause of death. Can I view the body?"

"Are you sure you want to? It's not a pretty sight." Paul smiled.

"Son, I've had to pick up the bloody body parts of my friends in Afghanistan – do you think this will upset me?"

"I take your point, sir," said Rodriguez, showing a little more respect.

The air got cooler as the two men proceeded down the corridor towards the morgue. There was no-one there when they entered, the room was empty except for a gurney with a body on it covered with a white sheet. Rodriguez strolled over and pulled back the stained sheet as far as the shoulders.

In front of Paul, a mess of flesh, broken scalp bones and wisps of hair revealed itself, with teeth falling out of a broken jaw-bone. The white teeth provided the only clues that this pile of meat had once been human.

"Wow, it looks as if the pigs have had a feast. Perhaps he fell and couldn't get up quickly enough before the pigs got him. Is it possible to check any other cause of death?"

"It's difficult. The area we found him in is overgrown with broken branches – there are scratches and cuts from the twigs and sticks, some were sticking in him when we found him, there are lacerations all over the body. We will have to assume accidental death unless any evidence comes up to the contrary."

"I guess there's no point in an autopsy then?" said Paul.

"We've no reason to suspect foul play, and autopsies are expensive. I doubt my boss will allow one."

"Thank you. May I contact you again if anything else comes up?"

"Of course, sir, I'll be glad to help." They moved away from the foul-smelling body and the officer escorted Paul to the door.

"Who was that?" the curious desk sergeant also watched the white man walk away.

"He's a friend of Jinky, the widow of the old white guy that owned the Blue Room Hotel.

The one that just got killed." The sergeant nodded.

"Oh yes, I heard the was a new foreigner staying there. D'you think he'll be a problem?"

"No, I'm pretty sure he believed me."

"Let's hope so. Charlie would not be happy if a foreigner tried to cause trouble, none of us can afford to cross Charlie."

"Understood, sir. I'll watch him."

***

Maxwell's house was easy to find; a small but well-kept house in a street of shacks and tinder-block structures. The front garden boasted fruit trees, with all kinds of orchids hanging on the wall.

As Paul strode up the drive, a young woman came out carrying a baby.

"Can I help you?"

"Sorry to bother you, but does Maxwell live here? I'd just like a word with him."

"He's just gone to the store. Do you want to wait? I'm Marites, Maxwell's wife. You're Paul aren't you, Joe's friend? Maxwell heard you stayed at the hotel."

She showed him into a tidy parlor and without asking, brought him a coffee.

"How is Jinky? This is a terrible business, Paul. I still can't believe that Joe was stupid enough to go hunting boar on his own. He always asked Maxwell to take him."

"Yes, it seems out of character. Are you sure Joe didn't call here for Maxwell to take him up?"

"Oh yes, I'm sure. Maxwell stayed here all day with his friend Tony, I was working. I don't like Tony much – he gives me the creeps. He's a bad influence on Maxwell." "So, Maxwell and Tony stayed here all day? Joe didn't come round?"

"They were both drunk when I got home. It looked like they'd been drinking all day."

Marites thought it would be better if she didn't mention Alexander.

"Why don't you like this Tony character, Marites?"

"Nobody likes him round here. He's a nasty piece of work – he's one of Charlie's men. I can't understand why Maxwell hangs out with him. I wish he wouldn't."

Paul's ears pricked up at the mention on Charlie – things seemed stranger. Mention of

Charlie again concerned Paul. This was the second time the man's name had come up today in a negative way. He felt uncomfortable about this business.

"How do you think Joe got up the mountain, Marites?" She thought for a moment.

"I assume he drove up there. He's got a big car, a four-wheel drive, they always used Joe's car when they went hunting. It's a hatchback – easy to put the pigs in."

"The police said they didn't find his truck when they found his body," said Paul.

"Oh, that's weird. Why wouldn't he take his truck? Maybe his truck had a problem. He might have taken a taxi I suppose., but a taxi wouldn't have taken him deep into the jungle, and any taxi driver would have more sense than to leave him there."

"I guess we'll never know." Said Paul, finishing his coffee. He rose to leave. Marites called after him.

"Tell Jinky I'll call round, poor thing."

Paul said he would and left. Paul liked Marites, he considered himself a good judge of character – she seemed genuine to him. But he noted she was not at home when Joe'd gone missing.

As Paul's car turned the corner at end of the street, Marites took the ringing phone out of her pocket.

"Maxwell, where are you. That white friend of Jinky just came round. He wanted to see you. Get back as soon as you can, I don't like anything that involves Tony or Charlie. I hope no one will ever know of our involvement."

***

After a couple of days trying, Cute Ass got hold of Charlie.

"Where have you been? I've been worried, sweetheart."

"Just busy, love. It's all sorted now, so I'll be able to see you soon."

There's a lot going on here, did you know that Joe, the owner died? Apparently in a hunting accident. Jinky is so upset.

"I expect she is, it's a shame she didn't persuade the old fool to sell to me when he had the chance. Joe only had himself to blame."

Cute Ass was confused.

"What do you mean? Did you have something to do with his death, Charlie?"

"Look, sweetheart. This is business. It's best you don't get involved in my business. I have to do things sometimes, things you may not approve of. It's best you keep out of it. The less you know the better."

She did not believe what he was saying. Charlie was a gangster, she knew that, but never realized that his 'business' would bring things so close to home, affecting people she cared about.

She feared her boyfriend now, but her instincts told her there was nothing she could do. But if Charlie did this to others, what might he do to her if she crossed him."

"Sure, that's your business sweetheart. I won't ask again. I just miss you." Charlie softened.

"I'll call you in a while, love. Don't worry. This problem will be over soon and we can plan the wedding."

Cute Ass was not so sure about the wedding now, but perhaps if they married, he'd change.

"That will be great sweetheart. I'll be glad to hear from you." The phone clicked off.

The young girl stared at the wall as tears formed in the corner of her eyes. Her family would be ashamed if they knew who she'd become involved with, and she loved them so much. What Charlie needed was a wife, then he'd calm down, she reassured herself.

***

There was only one catholic church in Angeles, and it was busy, but the priest seemed obliging. Tuesday was the first day that the priest was free for Joe's funeral. It was a quiet day for the city, but it would be packed – Joe was a popular man.

Paul was happy. Perhaps when she'd got that over with, Jinky could start to move on.

Hundreds turned out for the funeral procession, and the church was overcrowded. A wake followed back at the hotel which they closed to the public for the occasion. The solemn band led the mourners from the church to the hotel, about a kilometre.

Officer Rodriguez attended, as did his boss, Captain Protacio. The captain came over to speak to Paul. He was the only person in the room not holding a glass. Paul thought this was strange.

"It's good to see you don't drink on duty, captain. I'm surprised to see your junior officer with a glass of wine. The rules seem pretty relaxed here." said Paul.

"Well, I never drink, but you're right about the rules. It's sometimes difficult to keep discipline in a place like this."

He glanced over at Rodriguez, now on his third beer.

"The lad was very helpful to me when I went to talk to him about Joe's death."

Paul observed the man's reaction.

"Paul, you've not been here long, and you're a foreigner. Many things are not what they seem."

The senior policeman moved closer to Paul and whispered.

"Be careful who you trust around here. Things haven't been the same since the triads moved in. They're everywhere, and no-one dares stand up to them. I do my best, but I must be careful, they've got many of my police officers on their payroll – I have a wife and family, and they know that. They know everything."

"You mean they run the city and there's nothing you can do about it? What about getting help from Manila?"

"That's what it's like in the Philippines. I can't get any help from my superiors, many of them are also in the pay of the triads. It's so bad I can't even tell a junior officer not to drink on duty."

He nodded over towards Rodriguez.

"I better not say any more now, but come and see me in private if you need to."

Protacio strolled away, leaving Paul to ponder his words.

Jinky sat in the corner with two her girlfriends who discretely moved away when Paul came over. He covered her tiny hand with his.

"How are you keeping up, love? Today will be the worst day. Things will start to get better after this."

She looked up at him, teary eyed.

"I'll be glad when it's over Paul. Come with me, there's someone I want you to meet." She turned to the side.

"Alan, can you please come over here?"

"This is Paul. Alan is Joe's eldest son. He's the only family member who came."

Alan wore a suit but was obviously a military man. He shook hands with Paul for longer than needed. Paul guessed him to be around thirty. Clean-shaven with a military haircut; he had the bearing of an officer.

"It's an honor to meet you, sir, Jinky's told me about you."

"The pleasure's mine son, your dad was a fine man. What regiment are you son?"

"Same as my father, sir, I followed my dad.

Can I ask you something, sir?"

"Fire away."

"My dad was meticulous in planning. When I was young even a picnic had to be planned the night before and checked off a list. It's difficult to imagine he could have done anything so stupid. There must be another explanation." Paul sighed.

"Is this your first time in the Philippines, son?"

"Yes sir, it is."

"Well you'll find things are very different here. You must be very careful what you think, and what you say. How long are you staying?"

"Well, I was planning on a week, but I want to get to the bottom of this – I'll stay as long as I have to – I have four weeks leave." Paul nodded.

"Now is not the time or place, son. I guess you're staying at the hotel?" Alan nodded.

"Let's chat over breakfast tomorrow. seven o'clock sharp. Is that okay?"

"Yes, sir. seven a.m. I'll be there."

Paul was getting a bad feeling about this whole matter – and his feelings were usually right. Quietly, he chatted to all the ex-pat soldiers there and got their contact numbers, promising to be in touch again soon.

By the end of the afternoon Jinky was looking very frail and having trouble holding back tears. He stayed downstairs until the last guest had gone, not wanting her to be alone.

"That's the worst part over now, love. You've got to move on, you can take it slowly. It's been a long day; you should get some rest."

Paul helped her upstairs and into her room. She was drained, and half asleep by the time her head hit the pillow.

***

The next morning Alan was waiting downstairs when the older man appeared promptly at six fifty-five a.m. Paul raised his eyebrows and smiled. "Glad to see you're punctual, son. But I expected nothing less." "Sir, yes sir. Always on time." Paul smiled.

"I appreciate the respect, but I've been out a long time, I'd feel much more comfortable if you called me Paul."

"As you like... Paul. I'm glad you're here to help Jinky. I never got to know her very well, but she seems like a sweet lady..." Alan hesitated, as if not sure whether to continue, but he did.

"Paul, I have some concerns about my dad's death. Some things just don't seem right."

Alan was a bright lad, and obviously in Intelligence or something similar.

"Go on, son." Paul was keen to see where this was going.

"I know my dad, Paul. He was old, but there was nothing wrong with his mind. We spoke at least once a week. He was sharp, and I know he still had his strength. He was throwing drunks out of this place two or three at a time. There's no way he would trip and let a pig kill him. There's more to this than meets the eye, Paul. Will you help me try to find out?"

Alan was a sensible lad, a clever lad. He was no hothead just trying to let off steam, he deserved a chance to do this.

"Okay, let's say that I help you. Where do we start?"

"There's something that's been bothering me."

Paul nodded. Alan continued.

"Three weeks ago, he mentioned that a local villain asked him if he wanted to sell the hotel, dad told me he was quite threatening, but nothing that he couldn't handle. Maybe it means something."

Alan had Paul's attention.

"Did your dad mention this guy's name?"

"Yes, he said it was Charlie. Does that mean anything to you?"

"I'm afraid it does, Alan. Let me tell you about something that's been bothering me. The day Maxwell was supposed to take your dad to the mountains, his wife said he was at home with a guy called Tony. She said he was not a very likeable guy, and he works for Charlie."

"I think we may need some answers here, Paul. Can you tell me more about this Charlie?"

Cute Ass bustled over to clear away the breakfast things and brought more coffee while they continued their intense conversation.

"Charlie is the big gang boss in town. He is a triad – that's like the mafia in the US. It wouldn't surprise me if your dad's death wasn't an accident, and Charlie had something to do with it. I think this guy Tony may have been involved."

"Yeah, it's beginning to look that way. We need to find out what's going on. Any suggestions?"

"I heard that Tony and some of Charlie's other guys drink at the Rooster Bar. It's just down the street. Nobody knows you here in town, why not go down there tonight? You can ask around. There'll be lots of young white guys there – you'll fit right in. But if you do go, be careful. This isn't America, there's no law here to protect you. If you get into trouble, you'll be on your own. I'll check if any of my old mates are still here in town – we may need help. Let's rendezvous here at breakfast tomorrow, seven am.

"Thanks for the warning, Paul. But don't worry, I can take care of myself."

"Sure, see you then. Have a good day." The two finished their coffee and left. Paul went to his room while Alan set off to explore the city and see what he could learn.

***

Roosters bar was new. It opened three years ago when the Mayor, having refused a license to everybody else, issued one to Charlie. Since the opening it quickly became 'the' place to be seen. It's ultra-modern design, neon lighting, exotic cocktails, and disregard for the law about closing at two a.m. made it popular with local millennials with money.

The bar opened at nine p.m. each evening and by eleven p.m. it was packed, even on weekdays. They served breakfast from six a.m. each morning and closed their doors around ten. They were the only bar in town to make a cover charge – one hundred pesos – their clientele gladly paid it.

It was just after nine, and the bar was not too busy when Alan wandered in alone.

"I'm looking for Tony, is he here yet?" The bartender stared at him. "There's a lot of 'Tonys' around here – do you have a family name?"

"No, but he works for Charlie." The bartender raised his eyebrows.

"Take a seat and have a beer. He'll probably be in later; I'll tell him you're looking for him."

The cover charge didn't apply to everyone. Tony and his party never had to wait at the door.

It was eleven thirty p.m. when Tony with two of his cronies strolled in. After a few minutes Tony left his friends and came over to Alan, wary of the fit young man who was asking about him.

"They say you were asking for me."

Tony kept his distance, sizing up the newcomer.

"I'm looking for a job, guard work or protection, I'm special forces, but my girlfriend lives here. They tell me Charlie's the best hope for employment and that you're the man to talk to. Is that right?"

Tony relaxed now, there was no trouble here.

"Well, the boss is always looking for staff, maybe we could do with a foreigner on the team. Tell me about yourself."

"Not much to tell really, nine years in, active service in Iraq, ended up in special ops before discharge."

"Why were you discharged?"

"I was fucking the captain's wife, and he caught me."

"I didn't think that would be a sacking offense?"

"It isn't, but punching an officer is." Tony laughed.

Alan hoped he was convincing.

"Was she worth it?" Asked Tony.

"She was a good fuck, and I wasn't the only one fucking her, but I wish I hadn't punched her husband."

"Really? Why?"

"I wish I'd killed him instead. The bastard reported me for topping a guy in Iraq, I said it was self-defense, and they believed me, but that bastard officer had it in for me. That's why I punched him."

"Did he put up much of a fight?"

"Well, he started it; he came at me when I told him how much his wife liked it up the ass, which was true."

Tony laughed now, and slapped Alan on the shoulder.

"You're alright, you are. I reckon you might fit in well around here. Come over and meet the lads. Have a drink with us. They wandered towards the bar with Tony's arm still around Alan's shoulder.

"Lads, meet Alan, he's shacked up here with a local girl – wants a job. He's alright – give him a Red Horse."

Alan sat down with them, Red Horse beer in hand.

Tony was thinking how happy Charlie would be if he could recruit a soldier, especially a foreigner.

"So, what do you guys do for Charlie? Is he a good boss?"

"Well, you do pretty much anything he asks you too, no-one says no to Charlie. Sometimes it's collecting money, sometimes it's protecting the boss."

"Has he got a lot of enemies then."

"Look, he's a powerful businessman, and what he wants, he gets – and we're the ones who help him get it, whatever it takes. Sometimes we might have to get a little rough, I'm sure it's nothing you can't handle, and having a vet on the team will be impressive. The pay's good – that's why we stick around."

As the night wore on Charlie's men became louder, and more loose-lipped. One of the other two remembered something.

"Hey Tony, remember when we first got here, and the mayor needed teaching a lesson. The boss made you grab his little boyfriend and fuck him up the..."

"That's enough, boys." Tony cut in. "We don't want to frighten Alan off do we."

The other men were still giggling at the memory.

"Sorry, Alan, they can't hold their beer. Go on home you two, sleep it off – we've got a busy day tomorrow." They barely staggered to the door, and Alan could still hear them laughing halfway down the street.

"Tell me Tony, how dirty do we have to get, I don't mind the odd fight, but I've only ever killed people in battle, never in cold blood."

"You're in the Philippines now, Alan. Remember. Whatever you do, if you're working for Charlie – it's fine. No-one will touch you. The boss has the police department in his pocket."

"Do you have to kill people? I'm not saying I mind, just that we need to be protected, and the compensation better be good."

"Oh, don't worry about the pay, you won't be disappointed with that. But yes, you must do anything the boss asks you to do, without question. If you question him, you'll get yourself sacked, or worse. The boss is crazy sometimes. Anyway, you've killed before, just think of them as your enemy."

"Do you have to top them, even if they've done nothing wrong?"

"It's not up to you, Alan. The boss decides who's right or wrong – and you better go along with it. Are you having second thoughts? Because if you are, now is the time to say so and I won't take you to him tomorrow."

"No, it's fine Tony, I guess it will just take me a while to get used to how things are done here. Sorry for all the questions."

Tony became serious now, the merriment was gone.

"Make your mind up if you want in or not. It will reflect badly on me if I take you along and you don't join, you'll regret it if you don't join. Life will be difficult for you here."

Alan nodded. He didn't have to ask what Tony meant.

"Let me give you an example. A few days ago, the boss asked me to deal with a difficult old man who wouldn't do what the boss wanted."

"What did the boss want? How had the old man upset him?"

"The boss wanted to buy his hotel, but the stubborn old buzzard wouldn't even talk to him about it, and then we find out he planned to sell to somebody else."

"So, did you warn the old man off?" Tony laughed.

"What you must understand, Alan, is that respect is everything here, if someone disrespects the boss, there's no going back."

"So, what happened."

"The old man had to go. Charlie insisted on it. There's no need to worry, Alan. Whatever you do, the boss will have your back."

"You mean…"

"There was no risk here Alan, we made it look like an accident – everyone still believes the old fool got himself into trouble hunting."

Alan had to work hard not to show his burning hate for his father's killer. But he was self-controlled and disciplined enough to bide his time. He would get an opportunity soon. Tony continued, unaware of the change in the Alan's mood.

"Another good thing about working for Charlie is you can have any girl you want – nobody says 'no' to you if you work for Charlie. Wait, I'll show you."

Tony walked over to a young couple engaged in conversation at a quiet table and addressed the boy.

"May I borrow your girlfriend for a while?"

The boy looked angry and stood up. The girl caught his arm and pulled him back down. She hissed in his ear.

"Don't be stupid. Don't you know who this is? He works for Charlie. If you upset him, he'll kill you."

The girl stood up and followed Tony, glancing over her shoulder, she said "Wait there, I'll be back."

The boy sat there dumbfounded.

She moved away from the table, anxious that her boyfriend would not do anything silly. Inside she was terrified, but she needed to protect her man. Tony grabbed her arm and grinned at Alan.

"See how easy that was? Come on, you can have seconds."

The three shuffled their way through the crowded dance floor and out of the exit, Tony pushing the girl in front of him. Once outside, Tony guided the girl to the left, and into a shaded alley about a hundred yards away. It was a very narrow and dark space with a recessed doorway halfway down.

Tony pushed the young woman up against the door and kissed her. Alan watched Tony's hand working away inside her short skirt.

"You can do what you want, I don't mind, but you won't hurt him will you? He didn't mean any disrespect," the girl said breathlessly.

"Well let's see how much you please me, shall we?"

There was no point in fighting, but she hoped it would be over quickly. She opened her legs as his thumb moved between them. Alan could see the pain on her face as Tony roughly pushed harder.

"That's nice, now bend over."

Tony bent her over a trash can. He lifted her short skirt up to her waist to and pulled her briefs to one side.

Alan said nothing, but glanced around. Behind him was the back entrance to a fashion store – there was a box of wire coat hangers, some spilling out into the alley. Tony glanced over at Alan as his pants bulged with his excitement.

"See, they never put up a fight, and this one is nice, quite tight, I'll bet she hasn't been fucked much." Alan smiled at Tony, to reassure him.

Tony pulled down the zipper; he couldn't be bothered to drop his pants.

"Don't worry, I won't be long, then she's yours, and she'll be nice and wet for you."

Alan watched as the man became engrossed in trying to find the way in. She winced as he pushed at her with no lubrication. Suddenly Tony grunted, he was in. He turned away from Alan now to concentrate on his unwelcome actions.

Silently, Alan sidled sideways towards the box of coat-hangers and picked one up. Working behind Tony's back he bent it so it formed a large loop.

He moved towards Tony who was still engrossed in his sexual act. He was too busy to see Alan come up behind him until, in one movement, Alan slipped the metal noose around Tony's head and yanked it tight around his throat.

Tony gasped, and grabbed at his neck, but couldn't get a grip. He couldn't call out either. The wire crushed his windpipe. All he could do was gurgle as he sank to his knees. Alan twisted the wire tighter until it cut into the other man's flesh. Blood was dripping down onto the white shirt now. He kept turning the wire as it bit deeper into the throat. It took just sixty seconds for the man to take his last breath.

Alan was quiet, and quick. The man was dead on the ground and staring up at the night sky with an open mouth before the traumatized girl even realized anything was happening. She gasped in horror as she turned around. Alan was pulling the limp body into the doorway so no one could see it from the road.

Alan took hold of the shell shocked girl by the shoulders.

"Listen, you have to compose yourself. Everything will be all right, but you must go back in there as if nothing happened – you can tell your boyfriend nothing happened if you like. But you've got to get your boyfriend. Leave the bar straight away Hopefully no-one noticed the three of us leave, but if I were you, I'd leave town, at least for a while. The further away the better. Charlie will lash out when he realizes Tony is dead."

He held her shoulders and shook her gently.

"Can you do this? You mustn't show that anything's wrong."

She lifted her eyes and nodded.

He watched the girl run back up the alley before he ran off in the other direction and made his way back to the hotel by the back roads.

CHAPTER
FOUR

Alan Escapes

It took Alan less than two minutes to get back to the hotel from the bar, hiding in the shadows and alleys along the way. Jinky had given him a key in case he was late – he fumbled with the lock, but soon got inside the back storeroom. He shut the door and locked it.

He looked at his watch. Two a.m. now, but there were sometimes guests still drinking downstairs, so he tiptoed. He took his shoes off and padded up the stairs. Should he wait until morning to tell Paul? No, this was too important. Charlie would soon realize what had happened, and if anyone there remembered him from the funeral, they might tie him to the murder.

Things could happen before the morning. Very unpleasant things. He had to tell Paul.

He tried the bedroom door handle; it was locked. He tapped and whispered.

"Paul, wake up – it's Alan. I need to talk to you."

Paul was a light sleeper. Alan heard movement in the room and after thirty seconds Paul opened the door in his bathrobe, his hair unkempt.

"You're lucky I wasn't fast asleep – I had a few drinks and only came up thirty minutes ago, what's wrong?"

Alan pushed past him and closed the door. He sat on the end of the bed with his face in his hands.

"I'm sorry Paul, it all happened in a rush. I didn't mean for it to happen, but I've killed Tony, Charlie's man. I couldn't help it."

The distraught man sat on the bed and held his head in his hands. Paul pulled up a chair beside him.

"Alan, it will be all right. Take deep breaths.

Tell me what happened, son. Tell me everything, from the beginning."

It took Alan about ten minutes to relay the whole tale, then he looked up at Paul.

"What am I gonna do? They might be here any minute, where can I go?"

"Well, you're not going anywhere, not tonight. If you leave straight away, it would be very suspicious. They'd come after you. Let's hope for the best, they may not be able to tie you to the murder. You'll have to keep a low profile for now. Stay in here until we find out how the land lies."

Paul rose and opened the door to let Alan out.

"Go to your room, now. Lock the door. Sleep if you can. We'll meet up for breakfast at nine, but I'll fetch you. Don't come down unless I tell you. – let's keep things looking as normal as possible."

After Alan returned to his room Paul crept downstairs and checked all the doors. Just to be safe.

By eight, Paul sat drinking his first cup of tea, and scribbling in his notebook. Cute Ass brought over his food. Jinky sat down next to Paul, and spoke in a whisper, there were still guests around.

"We had a visit early today, it was only just light, Paul. That same young policemen who told me about Joe's death. He was asking if any foreigners were staying here."

"Did he show you a picture?"

"No, he just said he was looking for a young clean-shaven military looking man."

That's good, thought Paul, they don't have a photograph.

"I didn't tell them about Alan, I didn't think of him, he's family – I'm sure they couldn't be searching for him."

"I'm sure you're right, Jinky, but you did the right thing. We can't trust the police here, most of them are in the pay of that gangster, Charlie. I think we must keep Alan out of sight for a while, just in case." Jinky looked puzzled.

"Just in case of what? Is there something you're not telling me, Paul?"

Paul sighed; she'd have to be told eventually, better sooner. The place was quiet now, the guests had gone.

"Jinky. I'm sorry to have to tell you, but you're going to find out, and it's better from me. Joe's death wasn't an accident – they murdered him."

Jinky's mouth fell wide open, but she recovered quickly and glanced around and whispered.

"I'm not surprised, Paul. There's been something funny about this all the way through. I never believed Joe would be so silly. Who would want Joe dead? Do you know who did it?" Paul nodded.

"Tony, Charlie's thug. They did it because Joe wouldn't sell the hotel to them. Somehow, they found out he intended to sell it to me, and Charlie was angry."

"Well, what are we going to do, Paul? No point calling the police here, they're in Charlie's pocket, but we can't let Charlie and Tony get away with it, can we? Is there nothing we can do?"

"Jinky, Tony's dead, we need not worry about him."

Jinky's mouth dropped open and her eyes widened.

"Oh, my God. What happened? Wait. Has this got anything to do with Alan?

"Yes love, don't worry about the details, but when Alan found out last night that Charlie's man, Tony killed his father, he took care of it, now we must look after Alan... and you."

"What about you, Paul? You're involved too – you've got to be careful." Paul laughed.

"I've been in situations a lot worse than this, I'm a survivor, don't worry about me."

"I'm concerned Paul. What should we do? I'm glad for what he did; how do we keep him safe? Should we send Alan home?" Paul nodded.

"Yes, and the sooner the better. I just need to make some arrangements. Alan should stay in his room for now. I'll talk to him. Perhaps you can take him up some breakfast. I have some things to do. If anyone asks, including the staff, Alan isn't here anymore."

After Jinky left, Paul got to work on the phone calls.

"Hello Larry, it's Paul, from the Blue Room hotel – remember me?"

"Of course, mate. How are you?"

"I'm fine Larry, thanks. Listen, we have a situation here and I need some help. I don't want to talk on the phone. Can you come round?"

"Sounds interesting, I'll be there in twenty."

Paul finished his coffee while he waited, and continued calling his list. A few moments later Larry bounced through the door.

"Larry Godwin reporting for duty, sah!" Larry gave him a mock salute. Paul smiled briefly.

"Sit down Larry, it's good to see you."

"Good to see you too, Paul. Listen, it shocked me, what happened to Joe. I was at the funeral, but I kept a low profile. I just couldn't think what to say to Jinky, but Joe deserved a better end than that. I heard he was about to sell up and retire. Why would the old fool go hunting alone?"

"Things aren't always as they seem, my friend," said Paul, "Let me tell you what really happened."

Paul explained everything to Larry, who sat back, stunned.

"Wow, only in the Philippines…"

"Yeah, but now we have a problem. We've got to get Alan out of the country before Charlie works out he's the one who killed Tony. It has to be today – Charlie's out looking for him already. they don't have a picture, just a description. What we need is a safe and very discreet escort to the airport." Larry smiled.

"Just like the old days. Don't worry my friend we can do this. Let me call some guys."

Paul went online to book an air ticket for Alan. They would have to move fast. It would take an hour to get there. The next plane leaves for the US in four hours; luckily, there were seats left. There was time, but there was no time to lose. He phoned Larry, who was still downstairs.

"It's set up, Larry, but we must leave here in an hour at the latest."

Cute Ass brought them over fresh coffee.

"Roger that. I've got a mate coming to help us. He's on the way. We'll leave by the back door. He has a taxi, we'll use that, it won't draw any attention."

"Excellent work. I'll tell the lad now."

Paul knocked on Alan's door and walked in. Alan was sat drinking coffee and watching CNN news on TV. He was pleased to see Paul.

"Morning Paul. I've not slept. How could I after last night? I don't know what to do now. I'm glad I killed that bastard, but I'm sorry for any trouble I've brought to you and Jinky."

"Don't worry lad, it's all taken care of, but you've got to leave straight away. You won't be safe in Angeles anymore. We must go now. Pack up your stuff and be ready in twenty minutes, can you do that?"

"Yes sir, no problem, shall I come down?"

"No, I don't want you to leave this room until I come and get you, are we clear?"

Alan nodded and gathered up his stuff. As Paul left Alans room, he passed Jinky in the corridor and guided her silently into his room and closed the door.

"We must keep this to ourselves for a while, but we're getting Alan out. He's a danger to himself and you while he's here. We're taking him to the airport. Now."

Jinky nodded.

"I understand. What else is there to do?"

"It's all arranged, love. When my friend turns up, I'll take Alan out by the back door and get him on his way."

Paul joined Larry, who looked at his watch The taxi should be on it's way.

From where they were sitting, they had a direct line of sight to the backdoor. Paul walked through to the back and opened the door so they could see when the 'taxi' arrived. All they could do now was sit and wait.

Cute Ass disappeared out of the front door as Jinky came down the stairs. She called after the waitress.

"Where are you going? We have to prepare the lunches soon."

"I won't be long, just a quick errand, I'll make the time up."

Cute Ass was a reliable girl, so Jinky let her go, but it was unusual for the girl to take any time off during working hours.

The streets were well aired now, and the sun was rising. People avoided being outside in the heat when they could, so there were few people around.

Cute Ass scurried across the street and down an alley opposite. Working her way along the back streets, she headed for the casino. Even though she wasn't expected, Cute Ass hoped Charlie would be there.

As she approached the back door she checked around, she was alone. The brief and hurried knock brought a swift response.

"I need to see Charlie now. Let me in. I don't want to be seen coming here."

Without a word the door swung open, and she slipped in. The rear entrance opened out into the beer cellar. The lighting was low, and the place stank of stale beer. In one corner were two tiny chairs, where the staff came out for a quick smoke. She sat down and waited; she didn't have to wait long.

The pretty bar girl had been seeing Charlie for more than a year now. He'd promised to marry her one day. They kept their relationship quiet. She'd probably lose her job at the hotel if everyone knew, and Charlie thought her position may come in handy, especially if it was a secret.

That's why they spread the rumour about her being married to a foreigner. People would not ask too many questions about her being on her own.

The double swing doors leading into the casino floor opened. Charlie strode in.

Cute Ass rose and met him. He encircled her with his arms and kissed her.

"I've missed you," she whispered in his ear.

"I've missed you too, sweetheart. Come through to my office."

Cute Ass pulled him back.

"No time for that now. I came to tell you as quickly as I could. The young white guy you're looking for – he's been at the hotel, but they're leaving any minute to take him to the airport.

"Are you sure it's the same guy?"

"Yes, I heard them talking. It seems like they're trying to get him out of the country. Alan is Joe's son, that's why he killed Tony."

Charlie was surprised how much Cute Ass knew – but he was grateful.

"That explains it."

He ran back into the casino, and up to the nearest guard.

"You, quickly, find two more guys. Meet me outside in the jeep...Move."

Cute Ass stood back and watched as the four men flew past her one by one, then quietly let herself out as the open jeep roared off.

Back at the hotel, a white taxi pulled up outside the back door.

"Let's go."

Larry made his way outside to wait in the car while Paul went upstairs to fetch Alan.

Paul didn't knock. No time for pleasantries. "Come on, lad. It's time to go."

The older man led the way downstairs and straight out to the waiting car. They both slid into the back seat. They were on their way.

In less than five minutes they screeched onto the main highway, half an hour later the airport was in sight. Inside the terminal building the board showed that the Pan Am flight to Los Angeles was boarding. Alan joined the line with Paul and Larry watching out behind.

Charlie and his cronies headed out of town towards the airport. They never built the old Ford Expedition for speed, and at ten years old it was struggling.

"Can't this heap of crap go any faster than this?"

"My foot is on the floor already, sir."

"Well get a move on, and give me your phone."

Charlie dialed and waited, then banged the phone on the dashboard – the man was taking too long, but eventually someone answered.

"Listen Manuel, I'm on the way to the airport now. There's a young white guy on his way. I need you to stop him, do you understand? I'll explain when I get there."

Charlie was well known at the airport. Several of the senior employees were on his payroll – it oiled the wheels of the smuggling operation.

The young air-controller had recently been promoted to chief, thanks to Charlie's patronage

"No problem, sir. What's his name? and what flight is he booked on?"

"I don't know his name, or his flight, but he speaks English."

"Okay, sir, can you send over a picture?" Charlie sighed, exasperated.

"I don't have a picture." The young man paused.

"Sir, we have a more than a thousand passengers through the airport every day, and three terminals. How can we find him? You haven't given us anything to go on."

Charlie's face reddened, and the veins on his neck stood out as they always did when he was angry.

"He's young, about thirty-five, cleanshaven, smart, military, but he probably won't be wearing his uniform. Get out there and find him. Remember what you owe me, fucking earn it!"

"Yes sir, I'm on it, sir."

The bewildered officer headed down from the control tower, not knowing what to do. There were at least fifty guys that matched the description Charlie had given him, was he supposed to stop all of them? This was impossible, but he had to make a show of it, you didn't say no to the boss.

On the departure floor there were five endless lines for outbound flights, he looked along them. Several men fitted the vague description, but what was he to do. They were all foreigners, and you didn't mess with foreigners unless you had to. Locals you could get away with, but foreigners caused trouble.

Ten yards in front of the frantic controller, Alan reached the gate. He hugged Paul and Larry.

"Thanks for everything, and please let me know what happens. I'm worried for Jinky – I'd like to come back when the dust settles."

"It's not been a pleasant trip for you son, you've lost your dad. But I know you're gonna be okay."

Paul and Larry shook hands with him and watched him go through the gate. The young controller looked on. No, it wouldn't be him. The boss didn't mention any friends.

Twenty minutes later the officer was still patrolling the departure lines when the green jeep screeched to a halt outside.

Charlie ran up to him.

"Well, any luck? Where is he?"

"I've been searching sir. But I can't find him. Look around, they all look the same. It's so difficult."

"Do you have any planes about to depart?"

"There's a Pan-Am flight to the US about to leave."

Charlie ran over to the Pan-Am desk and shouted at the girl.

"Pull up all the passports for the flight that's about to leave, come on girl, quickly." The girl glanced over at the controller who nodded that she should comply.

"You. Get over here."

Charlie shouted at one of his men. "Look through these and tell me if you recognize him."

They all waited while the girl brought up each passport in turn. It was a 747 with over 350 passengers. This would take time, luckily, about halfway through they found him.

"There. That's him. That's definitely him"

Charlie looked at the screen and took a picture with his phone.

"Where is this flight now?" As Charlie spoke a plane left the runway and rumbled into the skies, passing over the airport's glass ceiling as it did so. The girl pointed upwards at the plane, nervously."

The veins on Charlie's neck were pumping harder now, his eyed were thunder. He was shaking as he turned on the young controller.

"This is your fault."

"Look, I'm sorry sir, I really am, but it was impossible to ..."

The young officer hit the floor with a thud, blood trickled from his mouth. He opened his eyes, but decided he shouldn't try to get up for a while. At least until Charlie and his men had gone.

Charlie strode away from the scene, rubbing his bruised knuckles. Maybe all was not lost, he'd noted the young passenger's name and had his picture.

***

The hotel was bustling with lunchtime guests by the time Paul, Larry and the taxi driver got back. Jinky smiled with relief when she saw them.

"Come in, boys. Have some lunch, it's on the house."

The three men sat in the usual corner, Jinky came over and sat with them.

"Did everything go ok?"

"No problems at all, and now that he's out of the way, I think that will be the end of it. Charlie will give up."

"If you'd been here as long as I have, you'd realize that Charlie doesn't give up easily."

With the lunch rush finished, they allowed the staff a few hours off before the dinner and evening trade. At three p.m., just before the three men returned, Cute Ass slipped through the front door and down the side alley opposite for the second time that day, speed dialing the familiar number as she hurried through the street.

"I'm coming. Please wait by the door."

As she approached the familiar back door it opened. Charlie beckoned her inside, he'd just got back from the airport. He was still seething. She worried about him when he was like this. He could be dangerous. He sat in the only armchair in the room, it was faded red. There was a small side table. A nearly full bottle of Jack Daniels sat there next to a glass tumbler half full with whiskey.

"I was worried about you Charlie. Are you okay? Is there anything I can do?"

Charlie held her hands. He was mellowing now. Thank god for the JD; Alcohol always soothed him.

"Sure there is, sweetheart. I will not be left with egg on my face. This is not the end of the matter – I'm sure there's a way you can help, but I just haven't thought of it yet."

"I'll do anything for you Charlie. I love you so much, and I really want to be married. When this dies down please say we can get married?"

"Of course, we can sweetheart; I've told you that many times. We've got to sort out this mess first, surely you understand that." "I suppose so," she mumbled.

He'd forgotten to mention to her he was still married – that would wait for another day.

"Look darling, please understand, I'll marry you as soon as I can. Until then it's better if no-one knows. It's only for a while. You can help me and find out things if people don't realize you're my girl. I hope you understand. That's why we spread the rumour you were married and planning to leave the country. It's better that way, it keeps you safe as well." She nodded.

"Sure, I just hope it won't be forever."

"No. it won't. I promise." He led her through to his office.

"There's just one more thing. Is this the guy you saw at the hotel this morning?"

Charlie showed her the picture on his phone.

"Yes, that's definitely him. He's Joe's son. He came over for the funeral."

"Well, he'll be back in America soon, that puts him out of bounds. Our boys in the US won't touch him, they know better than to tackle the army."

"Well if that's it, put it out of your mind now. No use worrying about something you can't do anything about."

"Oh, I didn't say I couldn't do anything about it. If someone kills one of my men, I have to do something about it. People will think I am weak if I don't."

Jinky closed the door and sighed as the last lunch diner left. Paul was still nursing his coffee in the corner. She slumped into a chair next to him.

"Oh Paul, d'you think that's the end of it now? I hope so. I've got this hotel to consider, and my future. I don't know what I'll do. I'd love to retire, but I can't see anyone wanting to take this place on now."

"What d'you mean?"

"Well with the Triads, and Joe and everything else, who would be interested now. I guess I'm stuck here."

"If you want to sell and retire, I'll still take it Jinky, I told you I was still interested. I'll give you the same deal I offered Joe. I like the place. I'm not worried about those thugs; I've got enough friends around here. I don't need to worry about them." Her face brightened.

"Are you really serious Paul? I'd love you to take over if you really want to. I miss my family in Cebu now. They were too poor to come down for Joe's funeral. I haven't seen my mom for five years."

"I don't say anything I don't mean, Jinky. Get the papers drawn up. Let's do it. No need to wait."

That afternoon, Paul called his real estate broker, back in the province.

"Hi Monique, how is the sale going?"

"We completed today, Paul. As soon as we clear the check, I'll send the funds through to your bank. You should get the money in a few days."

"Perfect. Couldn't be better. Thanks Monique, you've done a great job."

A week later Jinky and Paul were sat in the dusty attorney's office. It was like stepping back in time. The old lawyer had kept his office the same for the last forty years. Atty. Garcia had worked for Joe and Jinky since they bought the hotel. He was one of the few local lawyers who were not in cahoots with, or afraid of, Charlie and his gang.

At seventy-six years old he was winding down his firm, which was only a sole practice anyway. He was sorting out Joe's affairs. Jinky would have a good army pension as Joe's wife, and with the money for the hotel she was set for life.

She was a Visayan, and she was planning to go back to her family in Cebu. Her father was dead, but her mother was still alive, and she had two brothers and many nephews and nieces. She could help them now. They were not rich, and life was a struggle for them.

Several sets of legal papers lay on the table in front of them, after a cursory glance at them Paul put a check down alongside the paperwork. They both signed all the forms and Jinky picked up the check.

"I can't believe this is for me." She smiled, but then looked sad.

"It's a shame that Joe had to die for me to get it." Her eyes glistened.

Atty. Garcia tried to lighten the mood.

"Well, Paul you're the new owner of the Blue Room Hotel. How does it feel?"

"Ask me in a week," said Paul. "And, if Jinky doesn't object, I want to change the name of the hotel. I think we all need a fresh start." "I've no problem with that," said Jinky.

"What will you to call it?"

"I've thought about it for a while, but I've not decided yet – I'll let you know.

"And what are you going to do now, Jinky?" the attorney inquired.

"I will hang around for a couple of weeks, just to show Paul the ropes. We've kept this quiet; the staff don't know about the handover. We will tell them tonight."

After depositing the check into Jinky's bank they made their way back.

"Say nothing yet, love. Pretend everything is the same. We'll surprise them after dinner tonight." Jinky smiled.

"Okay, Paul if that's what you want. You're the boss."

It was a weekday, so dinner was not that busy. At the end of the evening there were just five of them left. Paul, Jinky, Cute Ass and two more staff. Jinky called them over to sit around the biggest table.

"Okay, everyone, we have something to tell you. As of now, Paul is your boss. He owns the hotel. He bought it from me this afternoon. I'm going to retire, spend some time with my family."

Cute Ass, the longest serving staff member, was the first to speak.

"Wow, I didn't see that coming, but congratulations, Jinky, you deserve this after all that's happened."

"Thank you, I appreciate that. You don't have to worry about your jobs. Paul's not going to make any staff changes, are you Paul?"

He stood as she handed over to him.

"As far as I can see everyone here is doing a good job. I don't foresee any changes, at least not in the short term. After all that's happened, we need a bit of stability for a while."

After a celebratory drink the staff left just after midnight. They would be late getting home that night. Cute Ass would be even later, she had somewhere to go first.

Under New Ownership

Paul's first day as owner started well. The place looked just the same as he went down for breakfast. Jinky was still in bed, but Cute Ass was in charge. Paul could see ten customers. They were all regulars, no fresh faces. Cute Ass brought him over his usual meal without asking.

"Do we call you 'sir' now, Paul?" She smiled. He laughed.

"No need for that, Paul will do just fine. By the way, what do call I call you? I've never known your name?"

"Why don't you just carry on calling me 'Cute Ass'? I quite like it." "Who told you?" Paul was surprised.

"There are no secrets in this place, Paul, you'll soon find that out."

"Cute Ass it is then,"

The girl laughed and skipped off with a theatrical wiggle.

The breakfast crowd was thinning when Jinky came down.

"Wow, it's great not having to get up to see to the breakfasts. I enjoyed my sleep."

"Well that will be the first of many, Love. You're retired now. Make the most of it."

"Have you thought about what changes you'd like to make."

"Oh, there won't be many, but I want to sort out the name change. I think it needs a new start, maybe different direction. Parris Island Hotel – what do you think? It has military connotations – it's the name of a military training camp in the US, many of the US veterans here will understand it and it might attract more to come."

"I understand, Paul. It's no problem at all. The place doesn't hold good memories for me now."

Jinky looked around wistfully.

"Perhaps I'll come back to visit from time to time – but not for a while, I need to spend time with my family now, my mom's not getting any younger."

Paul put an arm around her shoulder.

"Well, you'll be welcome here anytime, you know that."

"If it's ok with you I'll stay until the end of the week, I'll fly back to Cebu on Sunday." "That's fine, love."

Paul moved towards the entrance door. "I've got to pop out for a while. Can you 'mind the shop' for me?

There was only one sign writer in the city, and Paul wanted nothing fancy, just a painted wooden sign, maybe with tasteful lighting. Most of the local businesses had bright neon signs, sometimes flashing, but that was not Paul's style.

Flashing neon signs would not impress the new clientele that Paul intended to attract. He showed the little old man behind the counter the computerized mock-up of the sign he'd made. Paul had already measured up. He would put it right over the old sign – quicker and cheaper.

"How soon can you do it? Paul inquired. "It'll be three days. Is that ok?

"That's fine. Can you bring it and fix it?"

"Sure, but I hope you don't mind paying before I start?"

Paul took out his wallet and laid out two thousand pesos, while the man wrote out a receipt. After Paul left, the old man's son came out from the back.

"Why did you ask the white guy to pay upfront, you usually let them pay on delivery?"

"Not this time, son. Word about town is that Charlie has an interest in that bar. There have already been killings. I can't be sure that guy will be around in three days to pay the bill."

The lad chuckled and went back to his work in the stores. Paul returned to the hotel, and to his room for a rest.

***

Charlie was on the phone. His day was not going so well.

"No dad, there is no need for you to come here, and I don't need you to send anyone. I can handle this myself; I just wanted some advice."

Charlie'd spent the last thirty minutes recounting the events from the time he tried to buy the bar from Joe. His father was not impressed.

"You've killed an American? I knew you were stupid, but I had no idea how stupid. What were you thinking? There's over fifty thousand vets in Angeles, and they look after their own. This will not be the end of this, boy. You must do something. They could wipe you out easily if you upset them."

"Shall I kill the old white guy that bought the hotel, Pa?"

"Of course not, haven't you listened to anything I said? Look, go and see him. Put the pressure on. Turn up with some muscle. He's not likely to be intimidated, but he may give in just for a peaceful life."

"What if that doesn't work, Pa?"

"Find some other way to get at him. He's got to have a weak spot. Family, friends; you've to show him you won't give up – but if you hurt him, you can expect a ton of trouble, and I won't be coming to help you out. You'll be on your own."

Charlie feared his dad. In the past he did not dare to go against him. Things were different now. He'd been the boss in his own patch for years. He should be able to decide. But Xi said nothing he didn't mean. He knew his father would leave him to his fate if he messed up.

"Go and see him son, find his weakness – but whatever you do, don't touch him. Start thinking straight, boy. Another Vet? And a marine? If you did that, you and your pathetic band of men wouldn't last twenty-four hours. Are we certain he owns it now?"

"I've got a spy in the camp there, I can trust her, she wouldn't give me false information."

"Well, calm down, boy, and deal with the situation, don't be weak, but don't be stupid either." His father put the phone down.

Charlie stared at the phone for more than a minute, *thanks, dad, for nothing!*

Many times, Charlie had planned to leave the 'family' and go out on his own; some of his wilder men encouraged him to do that. Today was one of those times.

The young triad and his dad were not on good terms. The old man had sent him to Angeles more to get him out of the way – he'd caused his father problems in Manila. He got out of the city just in time before law enforcement moved in. He was reckless then; his father thought having his own patch to run might shape him up. He was wrong,

Phone calls with his father often threw Charlie into a rage; today was no exception. In anger, he jerked the drawer on the right side of his desk open. The large Johnnie Walker Black Label rattled to the front. The two-liter bottle was half empty, and within an hour it was empty. Charlie was the only person in the room to hear the smash of glass as it hit the wall. Fragments lay strewn around the floor and amber streaks made their way down the paintwork, covering older streaks from earlier outbursts.

A backroom in the casino served as a meeting room but was rarely used. Charlie managed the business by giving orders, not holding meetings, but today was an exception. His six senior men sat around the dirty wood table. It was cramped. Boxes of beers and whiskey were stacked against the walls.

"Don't just shout at them, son. Take them into your confidence sometimes, they might have good ideas. They've got to know you're the boss, son, but don't be too unapproachable."

With his father's words ringing in his ears, he summoned them to the storeroom.

"You all know why we're here, boys. We've got an issue with that damn hotel. We must have it. It has become a symbol now – if we don't get it, everyone will know we're weak. We'll get other gangs trying to muscle in. We can't have that. The bosses in Manila and Hong Kong will send other guys, we'll be squeezed out. It's up to us to sort it out ourselves, right?"

The boys were bemused. The boss never asked their opinion. Now that Tony was gone, Alex was the only one left who had come down from Manila with Charlie, he knew his boss's father. He could see what was happening – it had the old man's stamp all over it, but he'd keep quiet. It wouldn't help to show Charlie up.

"Boss, I think this Paul is more powerful than we first thought, and how could we know Joe's son was around, it's unfortunate, boss, but we can deal with it." said Alex. One of the other men piped up.

"The only problem is Paul. We have to do something about him. What about his family, can we threaten his wife or children?" Charlie shook his head.

"He's split up with his wife, she's abroad somewhere. I will talk to the man. He may be a veteran, but he's an old man. He may just want a peaceful life. Let's try it, anyway. We'll meet back here tomorrow morning to decide what to do next.

He turned to the nearest aide.

"Alex, you come with me."

Alex and Charlie walked down the street towards the hotel. It was still early evening; the dinner trade was just beginning. Cute Ass cast her eyes down as the two men entered, she slipped into the kitchen at the back.

"I want to see the owner please." The bar girl did not know Charlie or Alex, but they looked tough. She would not mess with them.

"Come on in, gents. I'll tell him you're here.

Who shall I say wishes to see him?"

"Tell him it's Charlie. He'll know."

She tapped on Paul's door and waited. He came after a few seconds. He was already dressed ready to go down for dinner.

"There're two men downstairs asking for you. One of them's called Charlie, the other didn't say his name." Paul thought for a moment.

"Tell them I'll be down in a few minutes – give them free drinks."

They hadn't come to kill him. This was too public, but he checked the revolver in his jacket, just in case, and wanted to take one more precaution. He went back into the room and took out his phone.

"Larry, it's Paul. Listen, are you busy? Can you come and just sit in the bar with a drink? Those triad guys have come asking for me. I don't think there'll be any trouble, but having you sat there will even things up a bit."

"Be there in ten, don't start the fun without me." Paul laughed.

"I don't think there will be any issues, not tonight anyway. Act as if you don't know me. We'll chat after they've gone."

Paul descended the stairs and smiled at the men waiting for him, they rose to greet him. There were no handshakes, he sat down with them in the corner, He positioned himself against the wall, as they always taught him.

"What can I do for you gentlemen?"

"Paul, I've heard of the events here surrounding the late owner Joe. His death was very unfortunate. I've come to offer my condolences to his wife Jinky, is she around?"

"She's already left town." Said Paul.

He knew she wouldn't want to meet these men; he'd told her to stay in her room.

"Sorry to hear that Paul, anyway, our real business is with you. I believe you own the place now?"

"News travels fast, I've hardly got my feet in the door yet, but yes, I bought it last week."

"Not sure if you've heard of me, Paul. The name's Charlie. I represent international investors here. We've built up a sizeable portfolio in Angeles. Casinos, bars, and many other high-end businesses. We're on good terms with the Mayor and get licenses pretty much whenever we want." "I see," said Paul.

"And what does this have to do with me?"

"The thing is, this nice little hotel would fit right in with our other investments. I hope we can convince you to sell to us. We'd offer you a fair price."

"Well, thanks for coming to me, I appreciate the interest, but I've only just taken over the place. It's not for sale I'm afraid. There are a lot of changes I want to make. I'll invite you to the party when I've finished."

Charlie ignored Paul's comments.

"We can make it worth your while, Paul. My investors have deep pockets, and frankly, they are used to getting their own way. The group is worldwide you know, with fingers in every pie. You'll have a quieter life if you consider their offer. You really should at least give it some thought."

At that moment Larry walked in, he glanced over at the others but didn't make eye contact. He settled in the far corner, Cute Ass brought him a beer, then went back behind the counter and picked up her phone.

Charlie's phone pinged.

That guy is one of Paul's men – be careful.

Charlie looked at his phone and put it down.

"Sorry about that, but we always have to deal with business, don't we?"

"Oh, I understand that. No problem, but I think you've wasted your time today. I'm not selling. Your group may be big and powerful, but I'm not without support. I'm ex-military; Vets stick together. Have you heard the phrase 'Semper Fi'? You should look it up. There are thousands of vets here. I don't need time to consider your offer. The answer is, thanks, but no thanks."

Charlie and Alex stood, there was nothing more to say. As they left Paul called after them.

"Good day, gentlemen. I'm sorry you've had a wasted journey. Oh, and I believe we should offer condolences to you as well. I heard you lost someone in a nightclub accident. That's very sad."

Charlies expression changed. His face looked like thunder. He turned to go back towards Paul, Alex just managed to catch him and pull him back. Paul returned to the bar and sat down with Larry.

"I guess you heard all that?

"Every word. They look mean, but they're nothing we can't handle."

"I've heard they have about thirty guys here."

"Well we can easily get together ten times that in the blink of an eye." Paul nodded.

"I know that, but if these guys want to, they can pull in men from Manila, and they've got the police in their pocket."

"I'd be surprised if things got that serious. It's just a tiny third-rate hotel (no offense)."

"None taken. Yeah, I think we could keep this local somehow."

"It's not as if we're after their drugs trade, is it?

"No, it isn't, but you may have given me an idea. Listen, I hope it won't happen, but we need to prepare for trouble. I'll bet there's more than a few lads living round here who'd help. Most of them miss the service." Larry nodded.

"Let's get working. If we sit down with a group of the lads and make plans, at least we'll be ready. Let's get them to a meeting and tell them the story."

They set up an operation room in Paul's bedroom. Jinky found an extra desk and brought it into the room. Now they both had a desk, phone, pen, and paper.

"We need to meet up with the guys, but a whole group of lads swarming around the hotel would draw attention. Can we meet at your place Larry? I know you've got a big place, and it's just outside of town. Charlie and his goons will have no idea."

Larry valued his privacy. He'd set his sprawling bungalow on a hillside to the north of the city. The next house was about a quarter of a mile away. It was at the end of a lengthy drive and hidden by trees. If many people turned up at Larry's place it was unlikely that anyone would notice. They had to act quickly. If Charlie was going to cause trouble, it would be soon – they couldn't afford to wait.

"See how many can come by noon tomorrow. It's short notice, but I think the lads will make the effort."

By midnight the list of promises exceeded one hundred men, and a few women.

"Let's call it a day, Larry. This is enough for today. I'll be out to your place by eleven, we have to prepare quickly."

***

Paul settled down for the night; there was nothing more to do. He made a mental note to bring Jinky up to date in the morning before he left.

She was already having her first coffee as he entered the breakfast area.

"Did you have a late one last night? I saw you were still talking with your friend when I went on to bed – it was nearly midnight then."

"No, we finished up soon after that, Jinky. Sit down with me for a minute, I need to talk to you about something." She sat down, puzzled.

"I had a visit yesterday from Charlie and one of his thugs." Jinky looked startled.

"Oh my God, I thought they'd leave us alone now. What did they want?"

"Same thing they wanted before – the hotel. They tried to persuade me to sell. They were not pleased when I said no."

"Perhaps you should sell to them. You know if you don't there'll be trouble."

Paul understood her concern, but there was no way he could back down and sell, even if he wanted to, which he didn't. He would do right by Joe, no matter what.

"Maybe, Love, but there's no way I'll give in to them. They're nothing but thugs and bullies. It's time someone stood up to them.

After all that's happened, I think I'm ready to take them on.

We must assume they will not go away nicely. Jinky, I don't want worry you, but it's better if you don't go out today, and try to find a place here you can hide, just in case there's trouble." Jinky nodded.

"My husband gave his life for this place. I'm not going to run away from scum like that. Just tell me what you need me to do."

Soon after ten a.m. Paul set off for Larry's house. To his surprise he was not the first to arrive. At least a dozen men sat on the porch surrounding the entrance and cheered as he approached, he hadn't been here long, but his reputation was growing.

Paul and Larry shook hands, laughing, and sat down. Larry brought out beers. Paul took him to one side.

"I appreciate the hospitality Larry, but it'd better if you don't pass any more beers out until we've finished our business. We need to be clearheaded for this."

The yard was filling up. It was thirty minutes after the arranged time, that was long enough to wait. There were about forty guys there. Paul brought them to order.

"Okay, lads, I want to tell you what the situation is, then what we propose to do, then – if you're still with us – we can work out the details."

They settled down in a group around Larry and Paul. Paul stayed on his feet and began.

"I expect you've all heard of the recent death of Joe Timmins, he owned the Blue Room Hotel. I'm sure many of you knew him. Well, I'm sorry to say his death wasn't an accident."

He had their full attention now.

"The Triads murdered him; they seem to control a lot of what goes on here. He wouldn't sell the hotel to them. It cost him his life."

Paul looked around; they were all focused on him. From the back of the crowd came a voice.

"So, we have to even the score, then – can't have the local thugs messing with a veteran, can we?"

The speaker was younger than most, maybe fifty. Paul nodded.

"Well it gets more complicated than that. Joe's widow has sold the hotel to me, and these triad guys are mad. I expect them to try something anytime."

"Any idea what they'll do?" said the younger guy.

"I think they'll come after the hotel, maybe they'll be after me, but I'll always be at the hotel, so it's the same thing, really. The first thing we need to do is work out a plan. Their boss is a Chinese called Charlie – he's a hothead. I think if anything will happen it will be soon. He's not one to wait."

"Understood, Paul. What's the plan of action then?"

It was the same young speaker.

"We need to protect the hotel. It could happen anytime; I met that guy Charlie and I don't trust him. He's a nasty piece of work. I see we have around twenty men here, there are a lot more coming later – we'll divide up into three groups and do twelve hour shifts. Who is available right now to come back with me?"

Paul selected six guys from those with their hands raised.

"Have you got any weapons?"

"Some of the men raised a hunting knife in the air, some men also had pistols, two had rifles.

"Okay, we'll take three cars, and we'll set out five minutes apart. We don't want to look like an invasion force. Larry, can you sort out the other two groups to take over later?" Larry nodded and walked off to organize the men.

Paul's car arrived back at the hotel first. He'd deliberately taken the two guys with rifles in his car.

"If you go up the back stairs, you'll see easy access to the roof. Find yourself suitable vantage points so you can cover the streets. Call me if anything happens."

They'd all exchanged cell phone numbers earlier.

The fourth guy was the younger man who asked a lot of questions. He only had a knife, but Paul thought he could be useful if it came to hand to hand combat. Jinky and the staff were watching the activity, Paul called them all over to the corner.

"It's okay girls, we're just taking precautions.

Nothing may happen, but we want to be ready in case. Charlie is mad because I bought the hotel, and he may try to cause problems. Don't worry, everything will be fine. We just need to have a plan."

"Shouldn't we close down or something? Are we safe here?" said Cute Ass. Paul nodded and smiled, putting a reassuring hand on her shoulder.

"If they come, they'll be looking for me, and maybe Jinky. You and the other staff have nothing to fear."

He glanced over at the frightened former owner.

"Don't worry, love. I can take care of myself, and you. We just need to make sure they can't get at you. I don't think it's safe for you to go out for a while. It's probably best if we let people think you've already left. Do you have any suitable hiding places here?"

"Well, there's the cellar." Jinky said. Paul looked surprised.

"I didn't even know we had a cellar, that sounds like an excellent idea."

"We hardly ever use it. There are hidden stairs. There's a trapdoor in the kitchen. Anyone can hide down there, and the trapdoor is difficult to see – especially if we stack some crates over it. No one would have any idea it's there."

"That's a good plan. At the first sign of trouble, we put Jinky down there and cover the entrance."

He looked at his watch. It was four p.m.

"Take a break now girls, the lunches are over. You must start the dinners in a couple of hours."

By this time, the other two cars arrived, and Paul positioned the men, some upstairs, a couple in the reception and two in the lounge, acting like customers. All they could do was sit and wait, and hope nothing happened.

***

Cute Ass looked around furtively to make sure she was alone in the back alley; she did not want to be seen going in. After two rapid knocks, the door opened, and she slipped in. The last time she met with Charlie he'd given her a key so she didn't have to knock and wait, but the door was also bolted from the inside so it wasn't much use. She could hear raised voices upstairs in Charlie's office. She called up to him.

"Charlie, I'm downstairs in the storeroom. You need to come down. I have information for you. I need to see you."

Upstairs, Charlie closed his phone and made his way down, shouting over his shoulder to the other men.

"I'll just be a little while lads. Get ready for tonight – it could be a busy one. We will let them know who's boss tonight, and avenge Tony's death. Stay here – I'll be back in a moment. Nobody leaves– is that clear?"

He looked around – all his men nodded.

Cute Ass heard a door slam above her, and footsteps on the stairs.

"You can't keep coming round here during the day, sweetheart. Someone will see you and report back to Paul, and right now you're better off as a spy for me – understand?"

"That's why I'm here. Paul's up to something. I thought you wouldn't want your men to hear this. If you go there unprepared, it will be an ambush. He's not stupid Charlie, he knows you're not going to accept his refusal without a fight, and he knows how angry you are about Tony's death, and letting his killer get away."

"Why, what has he said?"

"It's not just what he's said, he's been gathering other ex-pat veterans to support him. He's got some of them at the Hotel now. He's even got guys on the roof. If you plan to do anything, you better be very careful I'm scared for you, Charlie."

"It's good you came here sweetheart. That's useful information. We can make our own preparations now."

He moved as if to leave, but Cute Ass grabbed his arm.

"There's one more thing you should know. Jinky's still there. They're telling everyone she's already gone, but she hasn't, she's in her room. If there's any trouble they plan to hide her in a secret cellar. There's a trapdoor entrance in the corner of the kitchen. When she's in there they will cover the entrance with boxes."

Charlie was staring at the wall.

"So, she's still there is she? Paul lied to me. He'll regret that." He growled. "Ok, here's what you need to do..."

Cute Ass made her way back to the hotel. She was not looking forward to her shift that night. Jinky didn't deserve to get hurt. She sighed. She was in too deep now.

Charlie was deep in thought as he climbed the stairs back up to his office.

"We've got to re-plan lads. Paul has some help there, but we'll be ok – I have a contact on the inside. I know a way. This is what we're gonna do...

Cute Ass strolled into the hotel, deep in thought. She loved Charlie, but was not blind to his faults. She was just beginning to realize what his world was really like. If she wanted to get away, she'd have to plan it, and now was not the time. She'd have to go along with him. She consoled herself in knowing that Jinky would not be harmed. Charlie had promised.

***

Dinner service finished early, it was a quiet night, probably because it was mid-week. Paul and his boys were vigilant; the evening had passed without a major event so far. Just as Paul decided it was safe to relax with a beer, one guy on the roof called down.

"Maybe you want to come up and see this, Paul. Men approaching. They look like Charlie's men."

The streetlighting illuminated the otherwise dark road, it was nearly midnight, and deserted now.

"I think I'd better stay down here boys. I can see them through the window."

The three men sauntered down the middle of the road, just like a gunfight scene from an old western movie. They were not trying to conceal themselves or to act suspiciously.

The front doors of the hotel were still open. Paul and his friends pretended to be laughing and chatting as the men strolled up to the bar.

"Can we get a drink, please, miss."

"I'm sorry, fellas, we're just closing up. I can give you a couple of beers you can take with you. Will that be ok?"

The men gratefully accepted the drinks and left. Cute Ass followed them to the door and bolted it behind them. They didn't go far. There was a wooden bench opposite to the hotel entrance, next to the convenience store. They sat there to drink their beers and chatted, they seemed harmless, but this was strange activity for this time of night in this area. The youngest of the three had his phone out. He whispered.

"Sorry, boss, they wouldn't serve us. But they let us buy beers to bring out. We're on the benches opposite the hotel. What do you want us to do?"

"Just hang around outside, boys. Make noise, keep their attention."

The boy relayed the message to the others who laughed loudly and took another swig of their beer.

It would be usual at this time of night, with the last customer gone for the staff to leave and Paul wanted things to seem as normal as possible, he called Jinky over.

"We'll let the staff leave now, I'm not sure if anything is happening, but I don't want to take any chances. You need to get into the cellar. It's probably best if you spend the night there. If something kicked off there may not be time to get you down there. Just rest on the boxes – you'll be quite cozy."

"I'll help you," chirped up Cute Ass.

The two cooks were finishing up as the girls went through the kitchen. Jinky smiled at them.

"You can go now, boys. See you tomorrow."

One of the cooks bolted the back door as usual, then they left. Cute Ass quickly moved a few boxes and lifted the trapdoor.

"Watch your step, ma'am."

Cute Ass handed her a coffee she'd brought through with her.

"Here, take this. You may be down here sometime."

Jinky gratefully accepted the warm cup.

She descended the steps and switched on the single light bulb dangling from the ceiling below, making herself at home on some sacks in a corner.

"Ok, I'm fine. You can go now."

"Okay, Ma'am. See you tomorrow."

Cute Ass lowered the cover back into place, then stacked a few tomato boxes over it, concealing the entrance. She then went to the rear of the kitchen. Looking around to make sure no-one was looking she silently slid the back door bolt back so that anyone could easily open the door from the outside. Back in the front area she put on her coat and Paul let her out. He sat back down with his men and chatted. Relaxed, but ready. "There's two more of them coming." Someone shouted.

Paul looked out the window. This time he recognized one of the approaching men, he'd seen him at the airport with Charlie, it was Alex. They joined the others sitting opposite the hotel, smiling, and laughing.

Paul felt very apprehensive. His hunches rarely let him down; something would happen, but he didn't know what. The noises in the street disturbed him. A street party like this was strange.

One man produced a radio; the other men sang along to the tune. It wasn't a residential area so the noise wouldn't bother anyone.

Charlie watched from a safe vantage point down the street and smiled as his men laughed and joked. He speed dialled a number and raised the phone to his face.

"Okay, do it now."

He shut the phone without waiting for a response.

Three other men led by Alex moved silently from the casino and across the street, then down an alley and side alley which led to the back of the hotel. There was no streetlighting in that area, but still the men crouched and hid in the shadows, checking in all directions to make sure that there was no-one else around.

The others stood watch while the first man stood and tried the latch on the door, it opened easily. Alex slipped inside and looked around. He saw the stack of boxes in the corner and smiled. The other men followed him in, two of them moved the boxes away. The third man stood by the door through to the hotel lobby with his knife in hand, ready to deal with anyone who may try to come through.

They quietly pushed the boxes aside to reveal the trap door to the cellar. It was not heavy. The first man raised it without a sound and poked his head down to see inside. Jinky was sprawled out asleep on the sacks near the bottom of the stairs, this would be a simple job.

The two men descended the stairs and put the duct tape they'd brought with them over her mouth just in case, but she barely stirred. The drugged coffee Cute Ass gave her had done its work.

Jinky was a slight woman, and no problem at all for these men to carefully carry her back up through the opening and straight out the back door into the night. The last man replaced the cellar door and the boxes, placing them so that all seemed to be the same as before.

Carrying the girl between them, the men sneaked away.

Outside the front of the hotel two more men had joined the party, which was getting noisier, when one man took a call and nodded. He spoke with the other men. They suddenly got up and moved away, radio still blaring. Paul watched them until the turned a corner way down the street.

All was quiet now, as it usually was at two a.m.

"What was that all about." Said Paul, to no one in particular. "Shall we let Jinky out now?"

"No. It's safer if she stays there until the morning. I've no idea what just happened, but it might not be over."

At six a.m. the streetlights went off as daylight increased and people moved around the street.

"They won't try anything in daylight. I think we can relax until tonight."

Paul went through to the kitchen and shifted the boxes.

As he lifted the entrance door, he called down.

"Jinky, are you awake? It's morning now, you can come out. It'll be safe until this evening."

There was no reply. Paul went down the steps. It was a small cellar, and well-lit with the one light. There was no room there for anyone to hide. Jinky was not there. There was no hint she had been there, except for a coffee cup lying on its side, with fresh coffee spilled out.

"Jinky, where are you?"

Paul called out in vain. He rushed back upstairs.

"They've got her. I can't think how, but they've taken her."

Larry ran down to the cellar to check and came back up shaking his head.

"Paul, they must have found out where we hid her. Someone tipped them off; that's the only plausible answer. There must be a spy in here. We've got to find out who it is, otherwise, we're done for."

***

Staff started arriving now for the morning shift. Cute Ass came in first, as usual, and acted very surprised when told of Jinky's kidnapping, and of Larry's view that there we have a spy in the camp.

She began to panic. If they worked out she was helping Charlie it would go badly for her.

An idea crossed her mind, her instincts for self-preservation kicked in.

The new kitchen lad was next to arrive, he always came early to get things ready for the senior cook. No-one noticed as Cute Ass slipped into the kitchen behind him and shut the door.

"Good morning, you're early," she said, smiling and sidling up to him.

"I always get here about this time."

Her approach surprised the boy, she usually never spoke to him.

"Can I get you something?"

As he said the last word her hand entwined with his, what was this?

"Since you started here, I've fancied you," she said. "I've just never had a chance before." She pulled him in towards her and guided them both back into the pantry. He didn't resist, but her approach confused him. He looked at the door to the lobby.

"Don't worry, they're all upstairs. No one will come in."

She pressed her lips to his and opened her mouth. One hand snaked around his neck but with the other she opened the front of his pants.

He became too lost in what was happening to realize that her right hand no longer cupped his neck. He had often fantasized about this, but now, here he was with this gorgeous girl holding his growing cock.

As her left hand wound around him behind his back, her right hand picked up an eight inch knife lying on the table. At first it felt like a thump in the side as the sharp blade entered his body and pierced his kidneys. She pushed it deep and upwards, then left it in him.

He moaned, but she quickly tucked his penis back into his jeans. She covered his mouth as consciousness left him and he slipped to the floor. After zipping him up she reached in his pocket and pulled out his phone, entered a number in it, then dialed. It was answered in two rings.

"Charlie, it's me – don't call me back. I'll come over in a few hours."

She closed the phone then placed it in his limp hand. She found another knife and wrapped his other hand around it. Stepping back, she surveyed the scene, then, satisfied, she screamed and ran into the lobby.

Paul caught her as she flew through the door.

"What's the matter."

She was breathless, but blurted out

"It's the new kitchen lad. He tried to kill me."

Paul rushed through to find the dead cook staring up at the ceiling with his mouth open wide.

"What happened?"

Cute Ass could hardly speak for crying. Paul sat her down with a sweet coffee, she calmed a bit and tried to talk through her tears.

"I went into the kitchen and he was talking on the phone, I heard him say Charlie. I asked him what he was doing, he turned round and came at me with a knife, but he tripped so I had time to get a knife and stab him before he could get up. He came between me and the door so I couldn't run out." She started crying again.

"Well, it looks like we found our spy," said Larry, who'd been watching the whole thing.

"Perhaps," said Paul, not yet convinced.

"Does anyone have Charlie's phone number?"

"I have it," said Larry, "I bought a car from him last year."

He passed over his phone. Paul took the other phone from the dead man's hand and looked for the last number used. They matched up.

"Well, it looks like you've solved a problem for us, love. We owe you a lot. Larry, can you move the body, put it in the cellar and lock the door for now. We need to carry on as normal today. That will confuse Charlie."

Paul comforted the girl and told her to rest for a while. His thoughts wandered back to Jinky. They had to do something, and soon. Paul was thinking out loud.

"Larry, she's not dead. If they'd killed her, they would have just left her there." Larry nodded agreement.

"Where could they have taken her? I'm sure they're not holding her at the casino, they know we'd come looking there looking. I've got one idea. I'm going to the Police Station, wait for me here."

"Are you going to report the kidnapping?"

"No. No point in that. Half the cops here are in the pay of Charlie. I've just got a little business there."

He set off down the road just as the hotel filled up with breakfast customers.

CHAPTER
SIX

The Kidnapping

Several officers stood around talking with the sergeant behind the desk as Paul walked in.

"Can I see Captain Protacio please?"

"I'm sorry, he's not in yet. Is there anyone else that can help you?"

"It's okay, I'll come back later."

Paul seemed disappointed and started to walk out when Protacio walked through the door, briefcase in hand.

"Paul, what brings you here?" said the surprised officer.

"Can I talk to you in your office? I've got a slight problem I need your help with. When we met at the funeral you told me to come and see you if I needed anything – so here I am." The senior officer smiled.

"Follow me."

They set off down the corridor until the captain abruptly turned left into a sterile, but large office. The imposing desk and chair were offset by two chairs the other side of the room, and a small table against the wall with a plant on it. The clean white wall sported three certificates and a commendation.

A young female officer brought coffee in automatically as he sat down.

"We'll need another cup." The girl nodded and made off to the kitchen.

Paul settled into one of the guest chairs.

"I'm glad you're here, captain, there's noone else I can trust." The other man raised his eyebrows.

"I'll do what I can, Paul. What's the problem?"

"Did you know I've bought the hotel from Joe's widow?"

"News travels fast in this city, Paul. Yes, I had heard."

"Well, after the funeral, Charlie approached me about selling the place to him and I refused him. He got angry. Last night he and his goons kidnapped Jinky from the hotel. He didn't come himself, of course, but I'm sure he was behind it. I don't want to make this official – some of your guys can't be trusted." The man nodded.

"How can you be sure he's responsible, Paul?"

Paul did not want to tell the officer about the dead kitchen hand.

"It has to be him, there's no one else who would have an interest in taking her. She hid in the cellar. She could not have got out without someone kidnapping her. You're the only person I can think of who can help. I've got the skilled people here, I think you know that, but I've no idea how to find out where she is. Can you help with that?" said Paul.

The captain gave the matter some thought for a few seconds.

"I've got a few informers who are double agents, I can put some pressure on and see what I can find out." He looked at his watch. "Can you come back after lunch?"

***

As he arrived back at the hotel, Larry was waiting for him.

"Sit down Paul, let's think about this. As we see it, we have two problems, first, we must find Jinky and get her back. Once we find her, we have the expertise to free her, that won't be a big problem, but then what do we do? She won't be safe here; especially now. We can't risk taking her to the airport – Charlie will expect that, especially after your stunt with Alan. The first thing he'll do is have the flights watched. Paul, I have an idea."

Cute Ass brought them lunch while Larry explained his plan.

***

Paul returned to the police station at 2.30 p.m. The desk sergeant put him in the captain's office. Within two minutes Protacio rushed in. He looked pleased with himself.

"Paul, I found out where she is."

The policeman sat down and leaned back in his chair.

"If you're thinking of rescuing her, it won't be easy, and I'm not sure if I can help you.

I could try to do something from here, but Charlie will almost certainly know about it – this place leaks like a sieve. If that happens my efforts could do you more harm than good."

"Understood. Give me whatever details you can."

Protacio passed over a piece of paper. There was a hand drawn map and an address.

"She's being held there. It's a warehouse building on the outskirts of town. They bought it a few years ago. They turned it into a working bakery, their bread is actually quite good, but it is also a front. It has a big warehouse. They store drugs there, mainly cocaine, and other stuff they smuggle into the country. Cigarettes, Brandy, Motorcycles. Mostly from China, but often coming through Hong Kong."

"If you've known about this for a while, why haven't you dealt with this before, with your men?" Protacio sighed.

"These days I hardly know who 'my' men are. For others, their loyalties lie elsewhere. I'm working on it, Paul, but I'm not sure who I can trust here anymore. Some officers are paid by the triads, but there are some not in

Charlie's pocket. I've asked for re-enforcements from outside the town, but I'm always refused by my senior officers – I think many of them are also in Charlie's pay. It's a hard problem."

"Maybe I can help with that, captain. My guys all live around here, they have an interest in the safety and security of the city. Let's see what we can do."

"I can see where you're going, Paul. But be careful. I can't condone vigilantes."

"Who's talking about vigilantes?" said Paul.

"We're just concerned citizens." Both men smiled.

As Paul moved towards the door, the captain came over and whispered to him.

"Anyway, just so you're aware; at the back of the warehouse there's a small office. They built it onto the outside as an afterthought. The only way in is a door from the warehouse. There's no door on the outside, but there's a small window with bars on it. That's where they're holding her."

***

The car jolted to a stop. Jinky banged her head on the back of the seat in front. With the engine off the air was still and quiet, she was no longer in the city – it was too quiet. Roughly, they pulled her from the car and dragged her across a gravelly track and into a building.

There were unfamiliar smells, they were not pleasant. It could be tobacco, or whiskey, some mould and definitely old urine. They tied her wrists behind her back and blindfolded her. The car ride took about thirty minutes, but she was not sure where they'd taken her.

Two men were now pushing her forward over the dusty concrete floor. She heard a door creak open and they thrust her inside. She felt a tug as they undid her hands and took off her blindfold. A tiny shaft of light from the single small window high up on the far wall provided a little illumination. There was one chair in the compact room.

"Where am I?"

The two men did not even look at her: they left without a word.

She had no idea of the passing of time, they took her phone when she was still asleep earlier. It seemed like forever, but perhaps it was thirty minutes later when the door creaked open and Charlie walked in smiling. He handed her a bottle of water.

"Are you ok? I hope they haven't hurt you," she glared at him but said nothing.

"You guys have brought this on yourself. All you had to do was let me have the hotel. You could have had an uncomplicated life, and I would have what I want. We could all be happy."

Still she said nothing.

"Well. I think Paul will do the right thing now. You're Joe's widow, he won't see you harmed. As soon as he signs over the business to me, we can set you free."

There was still no response.

"Are you hungry?" she looked up.

"Ah, I see you are. There are pizzas outside. Shall I send some in?" She nodded.

"It must be twenty hours since you ate, Well I guess I can get you some nice food, as long as you do as you're told."

She frowned and spoke for the first time.

"What do you mean?"

He came towards her and took his phone out of his pocket and looked her straight in the eye.

"Jinky, you will do exactly what I tell you now. It will go worse for you if you don't."

Charlie needed her to comply with him while he set about recording her.

When he'd finished, he left without a word and she was left alone again. After a while a girl appeared with a large slice of warm pizza and a can of coke.

***

That night Larry put on his camouflage suit for the first time in twenty years. It brought back memories of his time in the army as a specialist in tracking, surveillance, and reconnaissance.

Set on a quiet country road, the imposing brick-built bakery stood alone. There were no streetlights around. Finding a place amongst the trees where he couldn't be seen was old hat to him. He'd been watching the entrance for a couple of hours now, making a note of the comings and goings. The old soldier captured all the activity, and he'd taken photos with his zoom lens. While it was quiet, he'd inspected the outside of the building, from a distance, and found the built-on tiny room that he knew housed Jinky.

The dense undergrowth went right up to the structure at that point so he could safely get close to the walls. He dared not call out to Jinky, she might not be alone.

The small window at the top was out of reach, but he examined the walls and took lots of pictures. After that he made his way back around to the front and set up camp. He had to establish how many people were there, their regular habits, how well armed they were, etc. His military infra-red goggles helped.

By four a.m. even from two hundred yards away, Larry could smell the comforting aroma of baking bread. It made him hungry. By six a.m. as the sun was rising, workers were loading up the three delivery vans with the freshly baked wares. Once the vans were on their way the bakers departed, they'd finished their shift.

Larry counted four men left behind, they were security. Each had a rifle slung over their shoulder. He noticed that one of them patrolled around the outside of the building every thirty minutes. The others usually played cards near the entrance gates. He had the lay of the land now. Time to report back to the hotel.

He joined the 'Council of War' at about nine-thirty a.m. The other three men were already sat around a square table in Paul's room. This meeting would not be public. Larry was pleased to see a plate of bacon sandwiches on the side and an urn of tea. He helped himself to both and sat down at the only empty chair.

"Okay, Larry. How did you get on? Is it doable?" Larry nodded and put down his mug of tea.

"The bakery protects the main warehouse, where they keep the drugs and stuff. The little room built onto the side is quite vulnerable. I have a plan, but we'll need a distraction, and we'll need some dynamite and a heavy-duty truck, an Elf would be ideal."

"When's the best time to do this?" asked Paul.

"Not at night. That's their busiest time. Morning would be best. After the bakers have gone home and the guards are tired. The day replacements come in at about ten a.m. The best time is around seven a.m. They won't be expecting anything, but it will be light by then - easier for us."

"Good work, Larry." Paul patted his friend's shoulder.

"Larry, can you get together the things we need? Then we'll all meet back here at six am tomorrow. Get some sleep."

That signaled the end of the meeting.

Paul had planning to do, but he could take a rest first. Just as he laid his head down there was a knock on the door. He called out for them to come in.

Cute Ass poked her head around the door shyly. She held a brown package.

"Someone just dropped this off for you." she said.

"Did you see who it was?" asked Paul.

"No. It was put through the door. I found it on the floor this morning when I went downstairs." Cute Ass responded.

He opened it in front of her and took out the small video cassette. Luckily there was a video player attached to the television in his room.

He looked up at Cute Ass.

"Thanks, love. Perhaps you can get me some coffee?"

"Of course, I'll be ten minutes."

Paul wanted to watch this video on his own. It opened with a wobbly view of Jinky's cell. The video was dark although Charlie had turned on the light, then panned down to a bedraggled Jinky who was slumped forlornly on a rickety wooden chair. Her eyes were red with tears. She looked up at the camera.

"Hello, Paul. I'm ok. They're not hurting me, but they've warned me that this will change if you don't give them what they want. Paul, I beg you to sell to them. You can never win against them. They're too powerful. Please help me, for Joe's sake. Agree to sell, so I can go home to my family. I hope you will..."

The video cut off and ended. Paul knew she would not say those words unless she was very frightened. Just at that minute there was a knock on the door and Cute Ass walked in with tray of coffee and biscuits. Paul looked up from the blank screen.

"Thank you, just put it down on the table."

Cute Ass put the tray down and started to leave.

"Wait a minute, can I talk to you?" She came back in and sat down on the opposite chair he indicated.

"Even when we get Jinky back, she'll join her family straight away. I need someone I can rely on when I'm not here. You've been here the longest and the staff respect you. I've been watching you – I think you'll do a fine job."

Cute Ass hadn't expected this, but she was pleased – it might make everything easier.

"It'll mean a raise, of course, and you must live in. You can have Jinky's old room. Is that okay with you?" She nodded and smiled. "Thank you for the chance, sir. I'm thrilled." Paul smiled.

"There's no need to call me sir now. 'Paul' will do. And what do we call you now – it's time we started using your proper name." Cute Ass giggled.

"Okay sir, thank you. My real name is Linda."

Linda grinned as she skipped down the corridor. At last she had achieved something that would make her parents proud. She'd have enough money soon to visit them soon. They were always in her mind.

***

Charlie answered his phone almost immediately.

"Paul's just made me manager – isn't that good?"

Linda was in Jinky's room cleaning and packing up the former owner's stuff as Paul had asked. She called Charlie as soon as she'd closed the door.

"That was quick work, He doesn't know what will happen with Jinky yet."

"Well, he's not planning on her coming back. I'm clearing out her room, and I'm going to move in here."

"He's clearing her room? Interesting. Did you give him the package?"

"Yes. I'm sure he's watched it but he has said nothing about it to me."

"Perhaps he plans on leaving her to her fate? Maybe he doesn't care about her. Either way we can't leave things as they are. It's gone too far now. There's no way we can let him live.

My dad won't like it, but I don't have a choice. I'll give him until tomorrow then we'll see,"

"Sure sweetheart. You know what's best. I'll help you all I can."

The words were automatic, but in her heart, she was distraught at how she had changed. Her parents would not recognize the girl she had become. She had not called them for a few weeks now – she was too ashamed.

"Can you get away tonight?"

"I don't see why not. I'll tell him I need to fetch my things. But I must get back to the hotel by seven a.m. I have to start breakfasts."

***

Jinky forced herself to freshen up. Soap and water felt good on her skin, and at least the shower was private. She hadn't washed for two days. Jinky felt human again.

On the way back to the storage room where they were holding her, Jinky thanked the girl again.

"That's fine ma'am. Try and get some rest. I'm off 'till later – I'll come and see you then."

The friendly girl started her shift at two p.m. – it was her job to clean the ovens and equipment ready for the evening shift.

During the day Jinky heard the sounds, and smelled the smells of the bakery, but saw no one, except for one burly guard who brought in a sandwich.

When the girl returned, Jinky was sat in the corner staring at the wall blankly.

"Are you ok?" the girl inquired.

"I think so. I hope I'm not here too long."

Jinky noticed the food that the girl carried, another sandwich. Jinky accepted it gratefully and ate it as if someone would take it away at any moment. In between mouthfuls she spoke to the girl.

"Can you take me to the toilet please? I don't trust those guards. Can you help?"

"We'll have to have a guard with us, but I can make sure they behave." Jinky brightened.

The girl stood guard outside the toilet, then walked her back to the room. Jinky was grateful.

"Thank you for looking after me. You're kind, not like the rest."

"I'm only here because I need the wage for my kids, I'm a single mum. I know what they do here, but what can I do? If I didn't do it, someone else would, and I need the money." Jinky smiled and nodded.

"I understand. What do you think they'll do with me?"

"I heard the men talking earlier. They're trying to force Paul to hand over the hotel to them. Charlie's wanted it for a long time, and he thinks he's losing face because he can't get it."

"What will they do to me if Paul won't give in?"

"Don't think about that, dear, they always give in to Charlie."

You don't know Paul, thought Jinky.

***

The old three-ton elf truck rolled to a halt outside the hotel just before six am. Larry jumped down from the cab and shook Paul's hand.

"I decided I'd bring this baby myself, seeing as how I already know the layout."

Paul walked round to the back. Everything was there – rope, chains hooks, sledgehammers, and of course, the dynamite. They all looked strong enough to pull down the sturdiest of buildings. A rickety old brick add-on should not be a problem.

As they went inside to wait a black Toyota land cruiser pulled up behind the truck. The rest of the hand-picked crew had arrived. Each of the five occupants wore battle fatigues, with balaclavas. Although not visible, they each had weapons concealed in their clothes.

It was time for planning and breakfast. Paul had cooked bacon and sausages – there were no staff there yet, and he couldn't find Linda. The plan was simple, but it relied on Larry's information being correct. He was 80% certain of his facts – that was enough for Paul.

"Remember lads, this is a simple extraction. I don't want anyone hurt, not on our side at least, and preferably not on their side either. There shouldn't be any need. Got that?' They all nodded.

By six-thirty they were on their way. They trundled separately and slowly through the deserted streets towards the outskirts – they were less noticeable that way. Once they were outside the city, they were on wider roads which were more open. They joined up again as they approached the Bakery. A dense thicket of trees and bushes spread like a crescent moon from near the front of the building to the back, providing sufficient cover for them. They parked up there, off the road, and out of sight.

One man took up position watching the entrance and the guard station through his binoculars, keeping his head down as a lone guard strode around the perimeter. He timed the man - ten minutes; the guard would have a coffee and a rest now – twenty minutes. When he reached the guardhouse again it was time. They had thirty minutes – it should be plenty.

Larry drove the truck further on round the side, still out of sight of the gate and entrance and parked it maybe fifty yards away from the tiny room holding Jinky. Larry had two others with him. Three would get the job done quickly, and Larry's presence would reassure Jinky - it might make things smoother. Everything was ready, all they had to do was wait.

All seemed quiet at the front. It looked as if there were only three men at the gate. They all sat at the table playing cards. There could be others, but if there were, Paul's men could deal with them. Two men set off, scurrying thru the undergrowth in opposite directions, each carrying three sticks of dynamite, each with a varying length of fuse. One minute, ninety seconds, and two minutes.

About a hundred yards from the main group the two men lit their sticks and threw them into the bushes close to the entrance, then scurried back to join the others.

It wasn't long before the first 'bang' rocked the air. The man at the gate jumped up, knocking over their card table and ran to the gateway, taking cover behind the walls. Then came the second explosion. The guards kept their heads down. After a few seconds one of them crept forward around the side of the wall and inched his way towards the entrance driveway. They let him get about five yards out before lifting their rifles.

The men either side of Paul each fired a warning shot over the guard's head. He hurried back inside the gate; all was quiet, until the third bang. Nothing happened for a few seconds, but suddenly the sound of a revving engine split the air. A jeep came roaring out of the Bakery compound with three men in it. It came straight towards the group.

"Tires." Paul shouted. "Hit the tires."

His men were already on it. Several shots again rang out; the tire on the driver's side exploded. Dust flew into the air as the jeep veered to the left and seemed to be driving away when the marksmen took action. Well aimed bullets took out two more tires and it juddered to a halt. Luckily the jeep was still close to the entrance gate. The three occupants took their chance, abandoned the useless vehicle, and ran back into the compound.

Round the back of the buildings Larry and his men were now at Jinky's cell. There was no need to hide as they were out of sight from the drama going on two hundred yards away at the gates. They had to hope that the activity in the front had drawn any men which might have been guarding Jinky to the main gate. Larry sidled up to the wall and shouted

"Jinky. It's Larry, can you hear me."

"Yes, oh, thank God," was all Jinky could manage.

"Stay as far away from the window as you can, all right? We're going to pull it out."

"Okay, I will."

Crouched in the corner, she looked up to see a metal hook came through the open window and clang against the bars and fall back down. In a few seconds there was a second try. This time the hook flew through the window and curled around two bars; it held fast.

While Larry was throwing the hook up at the Window, another man was busy fixing the end of the chain to the tow bar on the truck.

Larry took a sledgehammer from the back. The truck driver inched forward until the chain was taut. Dust rose from the window cement as the bars came away easily, bringing an extensive section of wall with them and sending debris cascading down. There was just a soft thump as bricks and mortar hit the ground; the vegetation was thick there, and the ground was soft. Larry hoped it would not draw attention.

That makes our job easier, thought Larry. Before the dust settled Larry was at the wall breaking away the remaining brickwork at the base with the hammer. Just as he'd assessed, the wall crumbled easily and there was soon an opening close to the bottom of the wall.

Paul peered through the hole, squinting against the dust.

"Jinky. Come on out love. It's safe now."

The startled woman clambered over the rubble and took Larry's hand to climb through the hole.

Joe packed the hook and the chain back in the back and handed Jinky over to the other men.

"Get her safe into the car, then let's get going."

The guards at the front entrance were now back behind the brick walls, and very confused. If there was an attack, why hadn't they come? Why were they waiting?

Back at the Casino, Charlie was just dressing; his phone rang.

"Boss, we got trouble here, better come quick, but be careful – there's men out there with guns and explosives. They shot up the jeep, but they don't seem to be coming in. We're pinned down. We tried to go out but they shot at us and blew up the jeep. They're hiding in the bushes; we can't see them."

"Bloody hell, what on earth's going on. Okay, I'm on my way, stay put. Make sure the 'merchandise' is locked up and secure, and send someone to the back to make sure the woman is ok, then report back to me."

As he spoke 'the woman' was running through the dense undergrowth around the building to the safety of Paul's car. She was flanked by Joe. Once he made sure she got there safely he returned to fetch the truck.

One of Charlie's men ran towards the back of the compound, he would find a dusty pile of rubble, and no prisoner. Through the settling dust he watched a truck pull away and head around the side to the front. Larry was driving. He parked up beside the Landcruiser, as the men were packing up. When they were ready to go, they fired two shots through the open gates. He didn't want the guards to risk coming out yet, then he and his men made their way back to the car.

When he saw Jinky, Paul came round to greet her.

"Are you ok, Jinky? Did they hurt you?"

Jinky looked pale and tense but smiled a little.

"No, I'm fine, Paul. Thank you."

Paul nodded and got out to see all his men safely on board one vehicle, then helped Jinky into the Landcruiser and jumped in beside her.

"No time to talk now, love. We've got to get you somewhere safe. I'm sure Charlie will know what's happened. He'll be bringing more men anytime now."

Both vehicles then headed out, taking a sharp turning right, away from the city.

"Where are we going?" asked Jinky, surprised.

Paul held her hand.

"Well, you won't be safe in Angeles now, will you? Don't worry, we've made other plans. Just rest for a while, try to relax, you've had quite an ordeal." She nodded and nestled back into the seat.

After about half an hour they pulled off the road and up a winding drive. It was Larry's house. There was a large double garage to the right. The Landcruiser slipped inside and Paul pulled the door shut. Larry continued up around the back of the house where he could park the truck out of sight of the road.

Everyone gathered in the large kitchen where Larry's wife, Ellen made coffee.

"You've come up in the world since I was last here," joked Paul. "This is a very nice place."

"Life's been good to me, Paul. I've got an excellent business, a wife and two kids."

Just as they spoke, a boy and girl around five years old ran through the kitchen laughing.

"They're twins," said Larry in response to Paul's unanswered question.

Larry was talking to Jinky who was nursing a cup of sweet tea to calm her nerves.

"You can't go back to Angeles, love; it's not safe. I don't know when it will be safe for you." Jinky nodded with a tear in her eye. Ellen put a comforting arm on her shoulder.

"Linda packed your stuff up into three cases – they're in the car." Jinky smiled a little at this.

"Right now, Charlie will be checking the hotel, although he'll know we wouldn't be so stupid as to take you there. He'll have men checking on the airport, but he'll think you left by road, and he doesn't have enough men, or power to set up road-blocks on all the roads."

"So, what will happen to me, Paul?"

"You're going on a boat trip love. Larry owns a fishing boat – it's quite big and fast. We can get you aboard this evening after nightfall. The docks will be quiet then.

"Where will you take me, Larry?" "Home, love, we're taking you back to Cebu. You can tell your family to expect you tomorrow morning." Jinky smiled and threw her arms around Larry.

"Thank you, thank you. I'm so pleased." She held him tight.

Just as the sun was setting, the three of them set off in the Landcruiser to take Jinky to the boat.

As they came out of the gate, they turned right towards the coast and away from Angeles city. Paul drove with Jinky next to him. Larry was in the back. As they reached the top of a hill and descended, they could see the sea. They weren't far from the harbour, less than ten minutes.

"Are you coming with me, Paul?"

"I'm sorry, love. I can't I'm afraid. Too much to do here. I need to get this problem sorted. I'll go back and stay at Larry's house tonight; I need to plan my next move. But don't worry, Larry will go with you, we can trust him – I've known him for years, and he knew Joe well. He has two reliable local crew – you'll be fine. You'll be with your family in a few hours." Jinky looked worried.

"Please be careful Paul, you do realize how mean and vicious these men can be." Paul laughed.

"They haven't seen how mean and vicious I can be yet, love. You've no need to worry about me. I've dealt with worse."

***

It was dark as they drove into the sleepy port. There were only a few boats there. The dim streetlights led them around the harbour to Larry's fishing boat, the 'Mary Jane.'

They pulled up alongside and Paul took the cases Linda had packed for Jinky from the back as the two deck hands hurried to stow them inside.

"There's a clean cabin in there, love. You can have a pleasant sleep 'til you get there."

"I don't think I'll sleep tonight. I'm too excited to see my family."

Paul stood on the dock and waved as the boat pulled away from the jetty. When it was far out to sea, he returned to the Landcruiser and headed off. Larry would get back from his round trip to Cebu about midday tomorrow. Paul would pick him up. He might need Larry's help for the next steps.

Just before he reached the house his phone rang.

"Paul, this is Linda. When will you be back? We've got Charlie's thugs coming and going like they own the place. We can't stop them. They just barged in and searched all the rooms. They scare all the staff. I'm worried they'll walk out. Can you come back? We need you."

"Well, no, but having them wandering around is pretty frightening. Customers are leaving. What's going on?"

"Don't worry, Linda. They won't hurt anyone. It's me they're after. I will stay away until it's safe."

"Okay, but where are you. Are you safe?"

"Yes, I'm fine. I'll come back as soon as I can. I'll ask a friend to call to make sure you're all okay, you remember Larry? He'll be there tomorrow."

"Can't you tell me where you are, Paul? We're all worried."

"No need. Love. It's better I don't tell you where I am. That way you can't tell anyone. It's better that way.

He didn't think Charlie would go as far as to try to force information out of the staff. But better to be safe than sorry.

Linda closed her phone and straightaway rand Charlie. He did not look pleased.

"I'm sorry Charlie, he wouldn't tell me, but I don't think he'll be back tonight."

Charlie said nothing. He was stone-faced but inside he was seething. All his men were out searching hostels, hotels, bars and anywhere else someone like Paul might hide. Right now, Charlie cared about nothing else. He had to get Paul.

SEVEN

Secret Plans

Paul arrived at the wharf just before midday the following day; he could see the familiar blue and white boat on the horizon. It would take about fifteen minutes to reach the pier. The rundown café was all but deserted but he sat and nursed a quite good coffee as he watched his boat approach through the window.

His phone rang, it was an unfamiliar number. "Hello? Is this Paul?" Paul was cautious.

"Who is this please."

"It's Protacio from the police station in Angeles City. Is that you, Paul?" Paul recognized his voice.

"Yes, this is me. What can I do for you captain?"

He heard the man sigh with relief.

"I'm so glad to get hold of you. I thought you might be dead. The triads have got their people all over the city looking for you. Charlie is really mad. I've got a man in his group; he is telling me that the boss is becoming irrational and uncontrollable. They're even more frightened of him than before."

"I didn't think he'd be very happy after we rescued Jinky, so I'm staying away from Angeles for a while."

"That's a good idea; I'm glad you're safe. You don't need to tell me where you are, but can we meet up tonight? Things have been happening here that you are not aware of. It must be somewhere quiet and discrete, and away from the City."

"Where do you suggest?"

"Can you get to Olongopo? It's not far. There's a fish restaurant there with a backroom. The owner is a friend; he's a Brit and we can trust him. It's called 'Mikes Bar' – in Harris Street, just off the center. It'll be a quiet night tonight; we won't be disturbed.

Come along about eight p.m. Is that ok?

"Sure. I'll be there."

***

Olongopo was originally a tiny fishing village. But grew larger as its next-door neighbour mushroomed because of the influx of foreign troops. Being just twenty minutes from its Angeles, it was popular for quiet breaks and fishing trips.

Paul finished his call just as the boat gently bumped the pier. The crew threw the ropes over and tied them around the posts to secure the docking. Larry bounced ashore with a smile.

"All went well Paul. She's away from any problems now." Paul smiled.

"That's good, glad you are back. We may have problems of our own to face here."

Paul told Larry of his conversation with the policeman. Larry was skeptical.

"Do you trust this guy?"

"Only so far, but I can handle him. Listen, there are problems in Angeles. Apparently, the triads are taking the city apart looking for me. I don't think they'll hurt the staff, but can you call in on the hotel and chat to Linda. I think they'd be happy to see your face?" Larry nodded.

They got back to Larry's house around three p.m. and had a late lunch. Paul looked at his watch, it was five p.m.

"Let's make a start, Larry. When you've checked the hotel, call me. I think yesterday was probably the worst, so it shouldn't be too bad. They must have found out by now that I'm not there. I'll let you know how I get on with the policeman."

Paul finished his coffee and by six p.m. he was well on the way to the meeting.

Olongopo was a sleepy coastal town. Away from the center, the shops and cafés were dowdy and dirty. There was little sign of life.

The sun was setting as he entered the main street. It's not a big town and it didn't take him long to find Harris Street. Mike's Bar was still dark with no signs of life. In fact, there was no one walking in the street, and only one other car, it was still early yet. At the first opportunity he turned off into a side street. It was little more than an alley, and he could park up at the end – the car could hardly be seen.

As he reached the bar someone opened the blinds inside. Paul stepped back, prepared for anything. Suddenly, light flowed out onto the street through the windows and the front door opened.

"Are you Paul?" Mike was a short and tubby, jovial man. Paul, relieved, eagerly shook his outstretched hand.

"Mike, pleased to meet you. Thanks for helping us. Things are difficult right now."

"Yeah, I've been told about the riots and looting going on in Angeles. I was going there tomorrow, but I think I may wait awhile."

Mike ushered Paul through the small café area.

"I've set up the room in the back, so other customers won't disturb you. Paul followed. Mike left him with a cold beer and closed the door.

They didn't have to wait long before they he arrived. Mike opened the front door to let him in. Captain Protacio bustled into the room and greeted Paul, then sat down. No time for small talk, Protacio had news.

"Paul. When we met at the station, I told you of the problems I had with the triads having a grip on the town, and my men being paid off to turn a blind eye."

"Yes, I remember," said Paul, "but that's a common problem in many cities now, and you said that your bosses were not supporting you to get it cleared up."

"Well, that was true, until the last couple of days. It's got a lot worse now. We've totally lost control. We had so many complaints of thugs bursting into businesses and homes –

anywhere they wanted, looking for you. Some tourists complained to the US Embassy and my top brass in Manila have got involved now. I'll have some senior officers and reinforcements on their way to Angeles from Manila by tomorrow, but don't pass that on to anyone – I want it to be a total surprise and shock."

Paul put his glass down and addressed the policeman.

"That's all well and good, captain, but where do we come in?"

"Well, let me explain, I need help from you and all your experienced vets. It can't be official of course, but I already know what you're all capable of. And after all we're on the same side, aren't we?" Paul looked up and smiled.

"I'll do everything I can to help. I'm already up to my neck in it, whatever you need, you've got. Ask away."

"Well, let me explain. One good thing came out of the chaos of last night. The cops who were in the pay of the triads were out all-night working alongside the thugs. They just left the station. None of us gave them any orders. So, we can tell exactly who is in Charlie's pocket, and who is loyal to us." He continued.

"In short, I've got thirteen men I can rely on, and twenty-three who are Charlie's men.

We're outnumbered nearly two to one."

"Okay, captain. So, what's the plan?"

Over the next two hours, the captain explained to them that forty experienced and well-equipped men would arrive in Angeles at three a.m. the day after tomorrow.

"There will only be a couple of men on duty in the station at that time, and I've made sure that they're my loyal men. The new men will have time to take control before the next shift comes in at eight a.m."

"Are you sure you can trust the new guys coming from Manila? They may just come and support Charlie."

"I don't think so, Paul. These men are okay, I think we can rely on them. We have to keep silent about this. If Charlie finds out, it could ruin everything. We can't give him time to prepare."

"I still don't understand where I come in." said Paul.

"Well. Firstly, I'd like some of my men to stay at your hotel, we have some beds at the station, but not enough. Can you find us ten rooms?

Paul nodded.

"As you will appreciate, this is a very fluid situation; I'm still working things out

"Can you be at the Police Station the day after tomorrow? I guarantee it will be safe for you by then. About three p.m.? Then I can explain everything."

"Sure, Captain. I'll be there," said Paul. "I'm glad somebody has a plan."

***

After the chaos of the previous evening, the hotel was quiet for dinner that night. There were few customers. Charlie had two men sitting inside, just in case Paul showed himself. It put people off from coming in to eat.

Larry walked through the door at about seven p.m. Linda looked up from cleaning glasses.

"I'm glad to you're here, Larry. It's been terrible here. We were all very frightened, but it's died down today. I hope there will be no more trouble."

"Oh, I don't think there will. Paul and Jinky aren't here – so there's no reason for them to cause you problems, is there?"

He smiled and nodded at the goons, who ignored him. Picking up a bottle of beer at the bar he settled into the opposite corner to the two men.

Linda went up to her room to prepare for the evening trade, if there would be any; her phone rang.

"Charlie. I haven't heard from you for a while. Are you okay? No, Paul hasn't contacted me. I doubt he'll ever come back here with what's been going on these last couple of days. Charlie, this is ruining business. The girls and me rely on tips and we're not getting any – nobody's coming in – they're too afraid of your men. How long will this go on for? Haven't you done enough now?"

Charlie was not used to being spoken to like this by anyone, least of all a girl. He slammed the whiskey tumbler on his desk so hard it shattered. Linda listened to the noise at her end and was so glad that she wasn't in the same room with him.

"It'll go on as long as I say it will." he thundered. "I don't need you to be like this now, everyone in this town has to do what I tell them, including you, and the quicker they learn that the better."

"I'm sorry sweeth…" The phone slammed down at the other end before she got the words out. Linda stared at her phone. There was another call she had to make, and it couldn't wait any longer.

***

Xi Wong had not heard from the boy for three days now. He'd tried to call twice, but the call wasn't answered. He was worried about what was going on in Angeles, Charlie might be his son, but the bosses in Hong Kong would hold Xi responsible for any problems, and this would not be the first time that he'd had to sort out one of his son's messes.

The old Chinaman was tough, he ran a great and growing business and had made enemies over the years – you couldn't help that in this line of work. People had to respect you and fear you. But it was easier all-round if people thought you were fair, and as long as they didn't cross you, they would be ok. Operating in this way, and ducking and diving, Xi had stayed alive – many of his peers had not.

He'd been on the wrong side of the law for most of his life, but his business empire was very big now, and over the years he'd become powerful. He was probably the most respected of the triad bosses in Manila. To keep the wheels of his interests well-oiled he donated to many top politicians, and just a few senior police officers. He needed favours from people in high places. He didn't know it yet but today would be one such occasion.

***

Police General Calunsag left the army last year. It was usual for retired top-ranking officers to be given plum political appointments when they were no longer on active service. Celestino Calunsag was no exception.

He was not from a well-to-do family, there was no 'family money' behind him.

This made him an easy target for mobsters who needed an ear in top places. His work for Xi had varied over the years, from closing unfavourable investigations, to turning a blind eye to unlicensed bars and locking up Xi's competitors - making sure they didn't get out alive.

A tall man, he was in good shape. cleanshaven, and with dyed black hair, he looked at least ten years younger than his sixty-nine years. The two men became friends, and they trusted each other.

Usually it was Xi who called him when he needed a favour, but today it was Celestino who called the Chinaman and insisted on seeing him personally, right away.

Xi sat behind an enormous oak desk, glass of whiskey in hand. He stood and walked forward as the general entered the room.

"It's good to see you, Celestino, it's been a while. How is the family?"

"Everything's fine with me sir, but I'm sorry to say there are big problems down in San Fernando. You need to know what's happening down there."

Xi's heart sank. What had the stupid boy done now?

"You'd better fill me in, take a seat. Whiskey?"

"Yes, I think I need one."

Celestino told him the story of the complaints to the U.S. embassy (it turned out there had been fifty altogether) who had contacted the Manila chief of police, Celestino's boss.

Triad thugs were terrorizing the town because someone killed one of them and the killer escaped. Gangsters kidnapped someone close to the murderer, but she escaped.

Angeles city was now in fear because the triad boss had gone mad and ordered the owner of a hotel he wanted to buy to be killed. The man had apparently fled.

"What the hell is Charlie up to Xi? I've been told to take men down to take over the station there and restore order. We leave in a few hours. What do you want me to do?" Xi reflected for a few moments.

"Celestino, you must do whatever you have to do, it's your job. But, don't kill Charlie. You can take him into custody. It will do the hothead some good to calm down for a while – just make sure nothing happens to him. He's family and I must protect him. I'm sure you would want your own family protected in the same way, wouldn't you?" The policeman nodded, ignoring the veiled threat.

"I'll report back to you regularly. If I can, I'll bring him back to Manila." Xi nodded.

"That would be the best thing, but hang on to him down there for a few days. I'll be coming down separately so I'll meet you there."

The general finished his whiskey and left. Within the hour he would meet up with his men to set off for Angeles.

Just as Xi was pouring himself another drink the phone rang. It was Linda from Angeles.

"Xi, it's Linda, sir. I must talk to you."

Charlie's father had met 'Cute Ass' Linda a few years ago on a visit to Angeles. She'd just started dating Charlie. Xi could see she was a smart girl, and that she cared for his son. He'd taken her aside one evening and asked her to monitor the boy and to report to him if anything happened that he needed to be aware of. He regularly sent her money secretly.

They'd had a chat about every two months, mostly cordial reports on activity in Angeles, but tonight she had to speak with him on more serious matters.

"Linda, I'm glad you called. I've been worried. I'd been expecting to hear from you before now, I'm hearing terrible things about what's going on down there."

"It's been mad here, sir, but yesterday it got worse. Charlie won't listen to anyone. He's got the entire city against him now – he's trying to kill another ex-marine. If he manages that, it will be the end of him. There are hundreds of former soldiers in the town, they'll kill him, sir."

"Okay, I already understand about the situation. I'm taking some steps, but I want you to try to talk to him."

"I'm afraid to see him, sir. In the mood he's in he could hurt me. He won't listen to anyone right now."

"Ok, well just try to find out what's happening, call me again later, would you?"

"Sure, sir, of course I will."

"I need to come down there, Linda. Things seem out of hand. I'm getting ready now.

Don't tell Charlie I'm coming."

***

Celestino Calunsag had not distinguished himself during his military career. He got his 'desk job' as a general in the police after retirement because his father was a prominent but not rich politician in the province, rather than for his skills. But it was a job where he could do no harm, and he'd stay loyal to the president.

He'd commanded men in the field before, but not in action. They tasked him to take forty men to restore order in Angeles. Shouldn't be difficult.

At two p.m. he strutted into the command room in Camp Crame. The officers, spotting him, came to attention and saluted.

"At ease, men; Is everyone here?" His deputy, a lower ranking colonel, confirmed they were. Four large transporters sat outside waiting to transport the men on the ten-hour journey to Angeles.

"You can expect to be there for a week, boys. We'll leave it in the hand of the locals as soon as we've cleaned the place up. Okay, load up. We'll stop in Bulacan for some dinner, then I suggest you get some sleep. We're aiming to arrive in Angeles by two a.m. Get some sleep. We will be busy when we get there."

The convoy trundled out into the busy Manila traffic. The general travelled in the front vehicle. Roads in Manila were always jammed, and the lunch hour traffic still clogged the dusty streets, but after an hour they cleared EDSA and slipped onto the Northern Luzon Expressway, they could make good time now.

"Okay, sir. What's the plan?" enquired the colonel once they were well on their way.

"When we stop, I'll call our contact in Angeles, a captain called Protacio. He seems to be one of the few uncorrupted guys we have down there."

"What about the station commander, Alvarez?"

"I'm afraid he's part of the problem. He's been paid by the Mafia for many years, that's why the problem has got so big. He's acted like he works for Charlie and the mafia ratherthan the City. Our first job will be to arrest him."

"Understood, sir. Who will we leave in charge?"

"I expect we'll leave Protacio, in charge. He seems like a bright and reliable guy. If all goes according to plan, we'll give him a chance to run the place –let's see how he gets on."

The aircon in the old police vehicle could barely cope with the heat of a Manila afternoon. Many men were already asleep by the time they pulled into a busy eatery just off the highway.

"Stay in the vehicle, men. I'll send someone out for the meals. It's cooler to eat in here, and it's a very busy place. People may ask questions about a convoy of forty armed police heading north – we must keep this operation as a surprise until we get there."

He dispatched the driver and another man to fetch food and tell the other vehicles what was happening. Whilst waiting for his dinner he called Protacio in Angeles.

"Captain, how are things there?"

"Hold on one moment sir," said the captain as he retired to his office and closed the door.

"Everything is fine here, sir. The atmosphere is a little tense though. The officers in the pay of Charlie are going crazy with this search. They aren't even pretending to be honest police anymore. The good officers who still want nothing to do with the Mafia are staying off work or keeping a low profile."

"Well, all that will change tomorrow. We plan to be there around two a.m. What's the situation with Commander Alvarez?"

"Alvarez is never here at nights, sir. In fact, I haven't seen him for a few days. I'm sure he does not understand what's going on here or what we're planning. He's giving Charlie's 'boys' full rein. Maybe Charlie has told him not to interfere."

"Understood, son. How many holding cells do you have there at the station?"

"Ten, sir, but they can each hold four men at a pinch. I've got three men on duty tonight that I know we can rely on; you won't have any trouble when you arrive."

"Okay, son. I'll call you about ten minutes before we get there."

"Very good, sir, see you soon."

"I just need some air," said Celestino to his deputy as he climbed down from the vehicle. The heat was oppressive, but he found a little shade in a Kubo set away from the main area. The phone was answered after two rings.

"Xi. It's Calunsac. We're on our way. We've just stopped for dinner. We'll be there in the middle of the night and take control of the station straight away. There won't be any problem. What time will you get there?"

"I'm leaving soon. You will need some time to sort things out. I'll come and see you around lunchtime tomorrow. Don't forget, I don't care what you do as long as Charlie isn't harmed. I suggest you lock him up as soon as you can – I'm sure you'll have less trouble that way."

"I agree, sir. That was my plan – we'll see you tomorrow."

***

As Xi put his phone down the others in the room became quiet. He'd called a meeting of his senior men to discuss the Angeles problem, he'd been on speakerphone so they could hear the conversation. He turned to the closest man, his long-term friend.

"Everything's in place, Michael. I want you to take over when we get there. Charlie will be out of the way. You'll take a couple guys with you, but I don't think anyone will challenge your authority," Michael nodded.

Michael Wan was a second generation Philippino, but his family were from Shanghai. He'd been with Xi for over twenty years and was part of his 'inner circle.'

When his Chinese family moved to Hong Kong many years ago now, Michael acted as a liaison between Xi, with his vast network in Manila, and Hong Kong. Contraband goods and drugs flowed into bigger cities in the Philippines. Notably Cebu, Davao, Loaog, and Angeles with increasing regularity, and with few problems. Money flowed back to Hong Kong – Michael made sure it all happened. He was the ideal man to take control of Angeles for a while, and to help Xi sort out the family issue.

Xi dismissed the others and stayed in the room with Michael. He moved closer and put a hand on his arm.

"Michael, I need your help. One reason I'm sending you to Angeles is because of your family connections. You've been with me since Charlie was a lad, you've watched him grow up." Michael smiled.

"You know better than anyone what a problem he's been to be over the years. Well, he's done it again. This fiasco in Angeles is all down to him. There is a lot of fence-mending to do down there." Michael sighed.

"You've done everything you can for him Xi, It's his nature. He's been difficult since he was small, and he'll never change now."

"I know, old friend. But this must be the last straw, I can't let this go on any longer. I'm also responsible to guys in Hong Kong, and even in Shanghai, you know that. I have to do something."

"How can I help, Xi, you're like a brother to me." Xi sighed.

"We need to calm the situation down, mend fences – then consider the future – I think you're just the man for the job."

"If that's what you want, consider it done. You can leave all the arrangements to me."

"Thank you so much. I will bring the boy back to Manila. Maybe I can control him a bit. Maybe a few years here will make him come to his senses – we must see."

Xi poured another whiskey and looked at his watch.

"We need to leave soon. Pack and get back here in a couple of hours and we'll go together. Oh, and don't tell anyone where we're going. I don't want Charlie to know I'm coming."

"No problem, sir, I'll call you back later."

***

There was no street lighting on the country roads in the province, so their dirty headlights were the only illumination in the pitch black; looming up ahead were the lights of Angeles city. Calunsac and his men made good time. It was one-thirty a.m. now. They'd be there by one forty-five. He called Protacio.

"Nearly there, we're a little early. ETA one forty-five a.m."

"That's fine, sir. Everything is set here. See you soon."

Protacio arranged it so that the three officers working with him tonight in the station were his most loyal. He called them into the conference room.

"I have something to tell you, and I couldn't tell you any earlier as it's been important to keep quiet, but now I have some news.

You all know of the chaos in our streets lately?" His men nodded.

"Our bosses in Manila will not put up with the way the triads are ruining our city any longer. They've decided they have to do something There are a group of senior officers and men who will arrive shortly and take over the station. We'll give them any help they need."

There was a stunned silence. Eventually one of them asked.

"What about the other officers, the ones that are Charlie's men in disguise? What will happen to them?"

"Well, we all know who they are, don't we? I've made a list. The new officers from Manila will arrest them and hold them for a while. It's better we let them handle that as they don't know each other. We'll decide what to do with them as we sort things out."

"Sorry to ask, sir, but what about Commander Alvarez? We know he's in Charlie's pocket, but he's your boss." Captain Protacio smiled.

"He won't be for much longer. Manila knows all about him. After tomorrow, I think I'll be running things here for a while." His men smiled.

"We're with you sir."

He looked around at the other men, who all nodded.

"When will the officers from Manila get here, sir?" inquired another man.

"Any minute. Get back to your stations and prepare."

No sooner had they left the room and returned to their positions than the glass entrance door to the station opened and the General marched in, followed by his men.

Protacio walked out to the reception desk. They shook hands and he introduced the new commander to his men. General Calunsac spoke.

"Thank you for your loyalty, men, it is much appreciated, especially at this difficult time. Has Captain Protacio told you what is happening?" They all nodded.

"Good. Well, we'll take over from here. You can go home now. It could be awkward for you, confronting your colleagues. Have a break, you deserve it. By the time you return things will be quite different."

"Thank you, sir, we're all very relieved that you've come."

The fresh men from Manila were coming in and exploring the offices. Four men took up position at the reception counter with four more in adjacent offices. Calunsac took Protacio to one side.

"Look, we want to get Charlie and his top men, but I can't take men to do that yet and leave you shorthanded here. I think we'll wait until the first batch of men are locked up. When the station is secure, I'll take a few to the casino. That's where we think he'll be – and he won't have so much support because his police 'supporters' will be locked up."

"Good plan, sir. I guess we just wait for the morning now. Can I get you some coffee?" "We can do better than that, son."

He smiled as a junior officer brought in the coffee and the chicken and rice meals they'd picked up at Jollibee before they entered the city limits. It was very welcome.

At five a.m. the General gathered his men together in the reception area. The early morning shift would start coming in soon.

"Right men. It's nearly time. If any civilians come in, take them straightaway into the nearest empty office, we may get some trouble this morning. Those reporting for duty may well have other weapons on them, not just their service revolvers. Be ready for anything. Make sure they are properly disarmed before you take them through to the cells."

"What happens if they resist sir? How far can we go?"

"Don't think of these guys as fellow officers, lads. They're criminals, and probably well armed. Do whatever you have to. Use lethal force if you have to."

"Understood sir."

"I hope that won't be necessary, that's why I want a big show of strength. Hopefully, they'll realize they have no chance and give in without a fuss but be prepared."

***

At first light a lone man came through the doors and approached the desk, looking bewildered.

"Where is everyone? Who are you guys?"

The imposing new officer behind the counter looked up and called the man forward.

"Officer Castro, (his name was on his uniform). Please approach the desk."

Dumbstruck, he followed the instruction.

"We are from Manila, we have come to Angeles because of widespread reports of disorder in the city, and of rampant corruption in the police here."

"What had that got to do with me? I'm just doing my job here. Where's Commander Alvarez? He'll vouch for me."

The sergeant at the desk ignored his protests.

"We're suspending you pending an investigation. Please put your gun and badge on the counter."

The shell-shocked officer slowly complied after looking around. There were too many of them for him to resist. Another officer came forward to search him. By the time they finished it they took a smaller weapon (from his sock) and a large bowie knife."

"You realize it's an offense to carry more than the regulation issue, don't you?"

The bemused office pulled his phone from his pants pocket and started to dial.

"Oh yes, and we'll have that as well. You won't be making any calls for a while."

The officer who searched him grabbed the phone from his hand and placed it on the table just as the sergeant was putting everything into a plastic bag.

By nine a.m. there were eighteen men under armed guard in the cells. There were five more expected, but anything could have happened to them, they were late.

The door swung open as Commander Alvarez strode through. He marched up to the counter. He looked around, not sure what he was seeing.

"Who the hell are you, and who are these other men? What's going on here? Nobody has informed me of any changes."

"Well you are informed now, Commander," bellowed a voice from the back.

It was General Calunsac. Alvarez stiffened and saluted.

"Sir, begging your pardon, but can you tell me what's happening in my station?"

"If you'd had your eyes open, you'd realize what was happening. There is no law and order in your city, Alvarez. We've come to restore it. Oh, and we know of your little arrangement with the triads. We'll be claiming all your assets as ill-gotten gains. It's over, Commander. You're not likely to see the outside of a prison for a while." He turned to the Captain.

"Get him out of here, he disgusts me."

He turned on his heels and strode back to his office without another word.

Alvarez fumed, but there was nothing he could do. He emptied his pockets and handed in his weapons and badges just like the others. Still protesting, they marched him off to join his comrades in the cells. General Calunsac sought out Captain Protacio.

"Come with me, captain. I'll take over the commander's office. How many men have you got you can rely on? We need to call them back into the station now, if they're not already here."

"Eighteen sir, why?"

"Divide them into four teams of four. I want the homes of these men searched – including the Commander. Seize any computers, and all documents and papers. They've been getting rich for years for their work for the Triads. We can't wait any longer – word of what we're doing is going to leak out soon enough. We must hit them quickly, and hard. It's payback time."

"Understood, sir. Once we do that the whole town will realize what's happening." his superior nodded.

"My men can look after the station with your guys. I'll take ten officers; we'll pay a visit on Charlie. I hope he's still none the wiser.

Before he left the general assembled his team, his best trained, in the conference room.

"Okay, lads. We're going to get the triads. I'm expecting about ten of them, so be careful. I don't care if you kill them, but watch out for this guy."

Calunsac circulated a large and glossy picture of Charlie around the room.

"Take a good look at this one. We must capture him alive. Understood? Under no circumstances is he to be killed. This is the prime importance. Again, we must capture him – not kill him. Do you understand?"

"Do you understand?" he shouted, by way of emphasis. In unison, they all responded.

"Okay, final briefing in the meeting room – this way." He led his men in and closed the door.

A floor plan of the casino lay spread out on the table in the center of the room. The building was rectangular with only two entrances. A very wide and public glass doored lobby fronted the busy street, and there was a small, almost invisible doorway in the back alley. The alley was over-shadowed, with tall buildings on all sides and they'd painted the door black the same as the surrounding walls. Unless you were looking for it you might miss it.

The building was two stories tall, with a flat roof. One spiral staircase led from behind the bar to the upstairs, and in the backroom of the second floor a small wooden stairway led up onto the roof.

The Police Station conference room was small, the policemen stood together and huddled around the plan. General Calunsac was pointing to different areas of the building with his baton. He looked at his watch.

"They're not open yet, so there'll be no public to worry about. The last thing we want is innocent by-standers hurt." The others nodded.

"It's only five minutes away, we'll go there by foot. Did you all bring your civilian clothes with you like I asked?" They all assented.

"Okay, now's the time to change. You three (he pointed to the three closest men), keep your uniforms on. It will be good to show some uniformed presence, but not too much."

Calunsac had sent an officer out earlier to scout the area. The front entrance had shops and restaurants all around, but the back was quiet. Piles of rubbish, boxes and skips littered the narrow space, an ideal place for concealment. However, an assault through the back door may be difficult, the door would have substantial bars on the inside, making it nearly impossible to break down."

"What's this here?" an officer pointed to a small square on the map, next to the back door.

"It's a toilet."

"And this dark line above it?" Calunsac squinted at where the man was pointing.

"It looks like a window." He glanced sideways. "George, did you notice a window by the back door?"

"No sir, but hang on, I took some photos." They gathered round the scout's phone as he flicked through the pictures.

"Here, look, there it is. I didn't notice it because it's so far off the ground. Maybe eight feet?"

"Just the height you'd have for a toilet," commented Calunsac.

"Right. We're going to need a ladder."

The station had a light aluminium ladder that would do the job. Two of the lads picked it up.

"Go out the back way, and move through the back streets, try not to cause any attention."

Charlie was still in his dressing gown, he was a late night, late riser type of guy. He sat on the couch nursing the first coffee of the day and staring at his phone.

"Damn. Where the fuck is everybody? Why is no-one answering their phone?"

He threw his phone across the room. It hit his man, Alex, who was sat on the other couch, in the face. He yelped, startled. Charlie shouted at him.

"Keep trying to get hold of Alvarez, find the men. I don't pay them to ignore my phone calls. Tell them to get here straight away – we need a council of war."

Alex nodded and redialed the first number.

Charlie started his second coffee when he heard a tap on the glass front door below.

Surprised, he stared down out of the window into the street. He had a full view of the entrance on the ground floor. He wasn't expecting anyone, especially not the ominous group of men that now stood patiently waiting in the street.

Three uniformed police stood in front. One of them held a clipboard and a pencil. He didn't recognize any of them.

"What the fuck is this? Ignore them lads. They'll probably go away. Don't show yourselves, let them think there's no-one here."

There were five men downstairs in the gaming area. It was a quiet time, most of the men would come in later. They all sat around a large table in the back room, playing poker. Two men were with Charlie upstairs. The casino did not open until six p.m. – they usually took a break now and cleaned and prepared the bars, kitchens, and gaming tables in the afternoon.

'*Tap, tap, tap.*' It was louder now. One of them had his face to the glass, peering inside. They would not go away.

"See what the fuck they want, but don't let them in. I don't know them. They're not my men." Charlie was irritated.

One of the downstairs men sighed and put his cards face down on the table, then strolled off towards the front door. The others followed behind to back him up. There were three large locks to deal with before he could open the large glass doors. He opened it just a few inches, enough to ask questions without letting them in.

"How can I help you, gents? We're not open yet."

His face was close to the glass, his foot prevented the door from opening further.

"Can we come in, please?"

The speaker was a uniformed officer, rank of sergeant. He tried to look as calm and efficient as he could.

"Sorry, the boss isn't here, we're not allowed to let anyone in while he's not here." The policeman nodded.

"Okay, but we're investigating a complaint of food poisoning. A couple of people are ill this morning. They say they ate here last night."

"Well, as I say – you better come back later, the boss has to deal with this."

"We'll do that, but we'll come back with a closure order. If you don't let us check the kitchens now, we'll close the place down until we can check, is that what you want?"

Charlie was listening from upstairs. There was something very wrong. Who were these people? None of his men were there. There was only one way to find out.

"Let them in boys, let them do their work. Just keep an eye on them."

The man on the door backed down as his boss's words resonated from above.

Charlie's men watched them enter and spread out as the door fully opened.

While the three uniformed officers gathered at the table in the front of the casino, the others were amassed at the back behind the building, as if they were waiting for their colleagues to inspect the kitchen.

Just twenty yards away in the alley; the team moved into action. The rear passageway was dark and deserted as they had hoped. They'd already leaned the ladder against the wall under the window and scratched a circle with a glass cutter.

'Ping.' One of the men in the alley pulled his phone from his pocket. The text was brief and to the point. All it said was 'Now.'

There was only room for one man at the top of the ladder. He'd fixed tape to the glass in the circle. A sharp 'tap' on the glass brought a 'crack' and the glass came away in the man's hand. Charlie's men were all at the front of the building and luckily did not hear the crack. The man on the ladder reached through the hole and found the window latch. It opened easily.

He climbed down the ladder, and a smaller, thinner man took his place. The window took a couple of minutes to squeeze through, but soon he was inside. He jumped down onto the concrete floor. It was easy to sneak out of the toilet, and then he was at the back door. He was hidden from view, but he could peer around a corner and see the gangsters and his colleagues facing away from him just a few yards away. He had to work quickly.

There were three large bolts at the top, middle, and bottom of the door. Carefully, so as not to make a sound, he eased each one open. He could not tell if the deadbolt was still locked until he tried to open the door. Fortunately, the handle turned and it swung open quietly. He was now face to face with his fellow officers and waved them in.

All the men got inside just in time as their uniformed colleagues were coming through to the back kitchen. Luckily, the five thugs still did not understand what was going on and were annoyed, but still relaxed.

The lead officer had an idea.

"Sit down lads please, there's some

paperwork to fill out. It won't take long."

Reluctantly they all sat back down, looking cross. This was all going to go so much better if they were seated. Quietly, the three officers circled the group, hands on their concealed weapons. The lead officer took out his pistol now and trained it on the unsuspecting group.

"Okay, lads. You're all under arrest. Don't get up. Put your hands on the table where we can see them."

The startled men froze, then one of them shouted up the stairs.

"Boss, it's a trap. Watch out."

The police all had their pistols out and the plain-clothed men came out from the back room, guns raised, to support their colleagues. Two men were running towards the stairs when the first shot rang out. The lad upstairs fired at the approaching officers, hitting the lead man in the leg. He collapsed on the stairs, but the second man carried on and got a better shot at the man peering down the stairs.

The second shot was more accurate – it hit the lad square in the chest. He toppled down into the staircase, blocking the way. Two more men came forward and trained their guns upward while they attended their injured colleague, and the limp body of the goon from upstairs was removed from the stairwell.

Two officers cautiously ascended the stairs, knowing there was at least one more man upstairs. As the first policeman reached the second floor, he caught movement from on his left. Someone was climbing the stairs at the back to get onto the roof. He got off one shot, it hit the man in the leg as he disappeared through the opening to the roof.

He followed up the stairs and outside onto the roof. Charlie sat with his back to an air vent. A pool of blood was growing around his right leg. As the man came towards them, Charlie threw his gun away to the right and raised his hands.

"Don't shoot. I'm unarmed and I'm not going anywhere, but you're gonna be in such trouble when your boss finds out what you've done."

Charlie sneered at the silent man still holding a gun on him. He looked down at his leg.

"You'd better get me some medical attention. I don't know what's happening this morning, but you're gonna be in real trouble."

The thugs downstairs were all in handcuffs now, with one man guarding each of them.

"Shall I call for a van, sarge?"

"No. We will walk them through the streets; we want the whole city to see what we're doing today. That's why we're here."

On the roof one officer was using Charlie's belt to apply a tourniquet to his bleeding leg, he looked pale.

"We need to get him some medical attention. I hit an artery. I've stopped the bleeding now, but he needs to see a doctor."

They eased him down the stairs to the second floor and then carefully down the spiral staircase. Another man radioed for an ambulance, then detailed two men to accompany the injured Charlie to the hospital. "The general won't be too happy, we had orders not to hurt this one." His colleague smiled.

"No, he said we shouldn't kill him, nothing about injuring him – he'll be fine." They both laughed.

Back at the station, the renegade officers were nearly all in now. The holding cells were full, but they'd got them all, except for a few who'd not reported for work. They were probably going on the run. Protacio had dispatched officers to find them.

General Calunsac watched the proceedings from his office with satisfaction, he called one of the men who'd gone on the raid into his room.

"Where's Charlie?"

"Got hit in the leg, sir. They've taken him to hospital. It's not serious, he'll be fine."

"Thank you, sergeant. carry on."

Shit, thought the General. Xi will not be pleased. But at least he's alive.

The clock on the wall told him it was just after noon. Xi and his men would arrive soon.

The word was out now. People watched the triads being marched to jail; the families of Loyal officers had raided the houses of the corrupt officers and seized computers, phones and other assets.

Under close supervision Charlie arrived at the hospital, he was very agitated. Through his sedation he still barked orders at the police officers who guarded him.

"Get the police commander on the phone, tell him I'm here. Tell him to come here straight away, he's got a lot of explaining to do."

Charlie dialed the commander's phone for the hundredth time – still no reply.

"Why have you done this? You and your families will soon regret this." He said to the attending officers. The senior man took one nurse aside.

"Can you give him something more powerful to knock him out for a while. He's making quite a disturbance." She nodded and walked off, returning with pills in her hand and a glass of water.

"Take these, they're for the pain," she said, handing Charlie the pills.

About an hour later, Charlie woke up. He was more comfortable now that the pain relief had taken the edge off and his leg was fixed up. But he had an IV drip in his arm and a heart monitor attached to his chest. He looked at his phone. Still no calls.

***

Xi and his men stopped for food just before reaching Angeles at Shakeys Pizza. Being lunchtime, it was busy, and they had to wait for a table, but not long. Ten US dollars works wonders with poorly paid restaurant waiters. While they were being taken to their table Xi made a phone call.

"Hi Celestino, we'll be with you soon. How is it going there?"

"It's fine sir, everything went well with just one unfortunate incident. I'm afraid that Charlie was slightly injured. Don't worry he's ok. They accidently shot him in the leg. One of my guys only saw his legs and didn't realize who he was. But we've packed him off to hospital to get patched up and he will be fine. As you'd expect, he is bewildered and angry."

"As long as it's not serious that's ok. It might even knock some sense into him.

Where's the hospital. I'll see him before I come to you. Also, there are a couple of other matters I need you to take care of for me. I'm getting Charlie away from Angeles; my boys are taking him to Manila, he'll be out of your way there. I'm leaving a close friend down here to take care of our business. He's a much cooler head, so I want our men released without charge. You know that Charlie has been the biggest problem, and I'm getting rid of that problem for you, so I hope you can do this."

Celestino knew he didn't have a choice.

"That's fine sir, I'll text you the address – see you later. Is it ok if I hold your men until you get here? They need to see you and their new boss – we don't want them doing anything silly." Xi agreed and passed his phone to the driver.

"Change of Address. We're going here."

***

Charlie sat up in bed, eating soup. He was subdued from the drugs, but was still startled when his father and Michael walked into the room.

"What are you doing here, dad? I was only brought here a few hours ago. How did you get here so quickly?"

"I was already on my way son. I didn't know you'd be injured when I got here. How are you feeling?"

"I'm fine, just a bullet in the leg, but it went straight through. It'll heal quickly. But we've got to get that bastard cop that did this, dad. I want him dead." His dad smiled.

"Son, there'll be no more killing. As far as I can see, you've only got yourself to blame. I came because things aren't going well here. You've terrorized the city. It's got to end."

"But they're making a fool of me. If they'd given me what I wanted, everything would be fine. It's not my fault, dad."

"I'm sorry son, you've gone too far this time. You've killed one army veteran and you're trying to kill another. It stops now. I know you're family, but I've got wider responsibilities. I've got to keep our family in Hong Kong and Beijing happy. They don't like what you've done, son."

"Well, I guess I can pull back a bit, let things settle down for a while…"

"It's gone too far for that, son. You will come back to Manila with me."

Xi looked over at his companion.

"Michael's come down to take charge here for a while. He'll stay here in Angeles and settle things down."

Charlie learned years ago that there was no point arguing with his dad when his mind was made up. Anyway, he had no fight in him. Maybe it was the drugs.

"I'm sorry, dad. I can see I messed up. Just give me a few days to tidy up here and… His father jumped in.

"You're going tonight, son. You're finished here. I'll get my men to take you straight to my house. When I get back there, we need to talk about your future. You can help me run things in Manila for a while.

Playing second fiddle to you, old man? That's not going to happen. Thought Charlie.

***

In the Police headquarters in the town just about a kilometer away General Calunsac held a meeting with his senior staff, and invited Captain Protacio to join them.

"Things went well today, gentlemen. I think we can congratulate ourselves. It could have been a lot worse." He looked over at the captain.

"You're in temporary command of this station, son. I intend to give you a promotion and make it permanent when I get back to Manila."

"Thank you, sir." The men shook hands, then Protacio spoke.

"What will we do with all the guys we're holding, sir?"

"I'm taking your former boss, Alvarez, back to Manila – he'll stand trial there. The other officers you're holding need to be tried as well. Once you've done a thorough asset search. I'm sure that all of them will have much more wealth than they can account for. Can we rely on the local judges, or are they in the pay of the mafia too?"

"Three of the four judges are fine. The other one is crooked. We've known it for years, but Alvarez stopped us from investigation him. We'll go after him now."

"Good luck with that, captain. I'm sure you'll do well." He turned and addressed the whole meeting.

"Gentlemen, I need to talk to the new station commander in private if you don't mind."

The others left the room. They were in high spirits, laughing and joking.

"Captain, there are two more things you must know before I go. Charlie had been your biggest, in fact your only, actual problem in the city, is that right?" Protacio nodded.

"You need to be aware of a couple of things, son. First, I don't want you to go after Charlie's gang here. Find a way to work with them. It was Charlie that was the problem. Now he's out of the way things will be a lot easier. A much older and more experienced man called Michael will take over – there won't be any more trouble as long as we leave them alone."

"Do you mean they are still free to run drugs, prostitution and all the other illegal things? Why would we do that, sir? We have them now. It's time to finish them."

Calunsac leaned back and sighed.

"The world's not black and white son, sometimes we have to accept what we don't like."

Protacio stared at the older man.

"You mean we let them carry on as before?" The captain did not understand and was getting angry.

"No, not as before. They will be much more controlled now. But even if we tried to stop their activities completely, they'd send more men in and we'd be back in a war again."

"Are you in their pocket too, sir?" asked Protacio.

Calunsac bristled and came around the desk to face him.

"Look here son, let me make this clear. Unless you play ball, I can't let you keep command of this station long. Do you understand? Charlie's out of the way now. He won't stand trial here, he'll be taken away tomorrow, to Manila. I'll take care of him; you'll never see him again. Be grateful and take advantage of this opportunity."

"But sir, what about the murders, all the other crimes? We can't just let him go."

"It's a compromise, son. We've given the triads here a bloody nose today, but you know how powerful they are. There is no point in having a war with them, is there?"

He put his hand on the man's arm.

"Look, son. I'm going to see you get promoted, and you get control of this city, I'm just asking for a couple of things in return."

"What things, sir."

"Well, for a start you must let the triads go. You may well not have any cases against them, anyway."

"I'm sure we will sir, we just need to investigate..."

"There will be no investigation, son. You will let them go. Do you understand me?" Captain Protacio was beginning to understand.

"Charlie won't be coming back here. They have a new boss now. He's a nice guy, easy to deal with. I'm sure you'll get along with him. I'll get him to come and see you."

"Okay, sir. Thank you, sir."

There had been rumors in the force for years about Calunsac's involvement with the mob. It seems they were true. He was working on both sides.

Xi Wong said goodbye to his son and left the hospital. He made his way straight to the casino. By the time he got there, Protacio had released the detained men. They were back at the casino, and wondering what to do. They'd let Charlie down, and his father, Xi, was coming to see them; they were not looking forward to it.

Xi banged hard on the glass door, startling the men. Two of them rushed to let him in. They started groveling before their boss came through the door.

"Sir, we did our best. We tried to defend the boss, but there was just too many of them." Xi smiled.

"Relax boys, I'm not here for that. I'm sure you did your best, but we have made some changes here. First, meet your new boss, Michael. He'll be staying here and running things now. I'm hoping things will be a little smoother from now on. I want some stability here for a while, I'm sure some of you already know him. No more dramas. Let's try to concentrate on making money and not all these silly side issues." The men smiled and nodded.

As Xi left, Alex' phone rang.

***

Xi had two more stops before returning to Manila. But before that he had a call to make.

"Hello Linda, it's Xi. I'm here in Angeles. Can I come over?" Linda was surprised.

"Sure, no problem coming here, sir. Paul isn't back here yet."

"Okay, I'll be there in an hour. Can we have dinner in private? there are many things I need to tell you."

"That's great, sir. Looking forward to it."

Xi set off down the road towards the police station.

As he entered, General Calunsac came out to greet him.

"Hello, sir, I hope you're okay."

"You did a superb job, Celestino – well done."

"Thank you, sir. I'm sorry about Charlie."

"It's ok. He deserved a lesson anyway, and it's given me the opportunity to get him away and keep him in Manila for a while. You won't have any problems with Michael. Are you traveling back to Manila tonight?" The General shook his head.

"I'll stay for a few days."

"Okay, just keep me informed, I trust you to look after our interests."

"I've put the deputy here, Protacio, in charge. I've had a word in his ear; he won't be any trouble to you."

***

The battery on Charlie's phone only had one bar; he would have to be brief.

"Alex. Thank god you're not still at the police station, listen. The old man wants to take me back to Manila. There's no way I'm going to go work with him. Come and pick me up here, find out how many men are with me – we'll contact them later. Come as soon as you can – dad's goons may come to fetch me, and I want to be gone before they get here."

Alex smiled to himself; the boss hadn't given up.

"No problem. I'm on my way."

***

Angeles City Hospital had seen busier times, but it was still the largest and busiest regional medical centre in the area. By seven p.m. things had quieted down, visitors had come and gone, the evening dinner round had finished.

Charlie had few belongings, but a large case with clothes and all his personal effects stood in the corner, delivered earlier while he was asleep by his dad's men. He stared at it; a reminder that his time in Angeles was over, at least for now.

Inside, he seethed. He felt cheated, and he would never forgive those who brought all this about.

A sharp tap on the door lifted him out of his reverie and back to reality. Charlie was shocked to realize his father's men had already arrived.

"You ready, son?"

Michael stood in the doorway flanked by two men. They grabbed the case and made off down the corridor with it. Michael sat on the bed with Charlie.

Shit, dad's men are too early, thought Charlie.

"You know, son. This may all work out for the better for you. A fresh start, a chance to prove yourself. Who knows what the future holds?" Charlie nodded and forced a smile. In his head he was considering the ways he might kill Michael, as painfully as possible.

He rose from the bed and shouted in pain.

"Michael, please get the nurse, I need more painkiller before I go."

Michael strutted off down the corridor to find someone leaving Charlie on his own in the room. He had to be quick, he hoped his phone battery lasted long enough.

"Too late, Alex. They're here. I'll make them stop at Jollibee – one hour – come and get me. Bring what men you can." He quickly turned his phone off before Michael came back in with a nurse. Even after a booster shot, it was difficult to put weight on his leg. Michael supported him and helped him out of the hospital. A black SUV waited outside.

"Can we stop for some food? I've had nothing in the hospital. There's a Jollibee on the way out of Angeles. Can we stop there?"

"Sure, that will be okay, I'm not coming with you. These guys will take you to Manila."

Charlie peered into the car There was a driver, with one other man inside.

They shouldn't be too much trouble. He thought.

Michael Takes Over

Xi Wong had one last visit to make before leaving Angeles. The hotel restaurant was filling up as he entered. It was busier tonight; there were no goons patrolling the streets, and many people had heard of the day's surprising events. Linda was behind the reception desk as the distinguished Chinaman strolled through the doors. She gave him her rehearsed smile. Charlie had already informed her of what had happened, though she wouldn't tell Xi that.

"It's a pleasure to see you, sir. Have you come to Angeles to visit Charlie?"

"You remembered. Good girl."

"I've arranged for us to have dinner in my room, if that's ok. It's more private there. We don't want the staff hearing our business."

Xi paused and looked around the place as he ascended the stairs. Yes, it would be good to own this place. He'd talk to Michael about it. Perhaps there was a way, now that Charlie was off the scene.

Linda was already sat at the small table, and as he took the chair opposite her, a maid entered and put steaming plates of rice with roast pork, a classic Chinese dish, in front of them both. Xi smiled.

"That's very thoughtful, it's my favorite food."

"Anything to please, I hope you like it. I haven't seen or heard from Charlie today – is everything okay?"

The old man's heart sank. No one told her what had happened. The news would devastate to her.

He told her gently, but her eyes began to tear up as he recounted the shooting of his son and his departure to Manila. By the time he'd finished, she was sobbing. He put his arms around her.

"It's ok, Linda. I understand how you must feel, but it could be worse. I'm sure he'll be back, and you can visit him in Manila. Anyway, I still want you to be here, more than ever now. You'll carry on being my eyes and ears here, I'm leaving new people here and they may need watching for a while. She held him tight and became calmer now.

"Thank you, sir, that's reassuring. You are very kind to me." He stroked her hair until the quiet sobbing ceased.

***

Paul was bored. It was nice staying with Larry, but he was keen for news from Angeles and eager to return. He spent his time reflecting his life, his mistakes, and his future. Long ago he'd understood and accepted the blame for all that had happened and hoped that one day he and his wife might be friends, perhaps he'd soon be able to talk to Dennis. He missed his son so much.

He put his coffee cup down when the phone rang. It was Linda.

"Paul, are you ok? When are you coming back? It's safe now. Charlie's gone."

"What's happened, Linda? Is everyone okay there?"

"Yes, we're all fine. I'll tell you all about it when you get here. Business is picking up again, but we need you back here to reassure the staff."

"I'll be glad to get back there, love. I want to get my plans back on track. I'll be there tomorrow morning."

"Oh, that's great, Paul. We'll see you then."

After the call, Linda dialed another number. Charlie was still not answering his phone.

***

As he drove the familiar route, all seemed quiet, back to normal; but Paul was wary – what had happened? Had his policeman friend Protacio's plan worked? He looked forward to seeing the man, but most of all he looked forward to being back at his hotel.

The breakfast service was now over, but the restaurant still had a busy air about it. Two couples sat at the tables in the front. As he walked in, there were several tables of friends enjoying their morning coffee inside. Linda was busy upstairs but came down straight away when she heard he'd arrived. "Hello stranger. It's good to have you back." She gave him a hug.

"Can I get you something to eat? Or coffee?"

"I'm fine love, I'll just settle back in – I'll get some lunch later. Come and sit down with me, bring me up to date. First of all, what's happened to Charlie?"

"I don't know all the details, but they have sent him to Manila, so his dad can monitor him. Charlie went mad when you left. His goons terrorized the whole city. Manila sent police down to replace the corrupt ones here – even the former commander here is in jail now."

"I wonder if there are any triads still here, and who may be in charge of them," mused Paul.

"Someone said there is an older man here now, called Michael. A much more stable man." Paul nodded.

"Ok. It looks as if things are more settled. I need a rest now; I'll go upstairs for a while."

Paul rose, leaving Linda to finish her coffee. Secure in his room, he made a call.

"Hello, captain. It's Paul. I'm back in Angeles. I gather everything happened according to plan."

Protacio was pleased to hear from him.

"Welcome back, Paul. Yes, pretty much. I'm running things now, and the Triads are more sensible. The new man is an old friend of Xi, his name is Michael. I believe he's a reasonable guy. You'll get along with him - he will be fine to work with."

Paul was a little concerned.

"I should meet this 'Michael' – where can I find him?"

"It's better that he comes to you – I'll ask him to come into the hotel."

Paul agreed, but wondered why Protacio seemed so positive about this new Triad boss. Why hadn't the police taken the opportunity to get rid of them altogether? Something was not right, Anyway, he certainly had to meet the man.

***

Protacio was wearing a smart modern uniform. He liked his new, bigger office, and the men were showing him respect. The troops from Manila left the day before, and he was under strength now he'd lost the corrupt officers. He was recruiting as fast as he could and had three more interviews this afternoon, but he didn't expect much trouble. Things should be fine.

All remnants, mementos, photos etc. of the previous station captain were now gone from the desk, a large colour photo of his police graduation now boasted pride of place on the wall behind his desk. On the brief walk from his house to the offices, he'd been greeted by many well-wishers almost as a conquering hero.

He was not a man to waste time. He'd called Michael yesterday and invited him to the station. Best to get things off to a pleasant start. Punctually, at ten o'clock, a junior officer showed through the new boss of the triads in Angeles. Protacio came around from behind his desk with an outstretched hand.

"Welcome to Angeles." The older man shook his hand firmly and sat down, smiling. The junior officer returned with coffee in mugs, which he set down before the two men.

"Captain Protacio, it's great to meet you. I've been told good things about you. Let me tell you what's going to happen now."

The captain was taken aback. This was not what he'd expected. What was the man leading up to?

Many conflicting emotions had gone through Protacio's head in the past forty-eight hours. He was not a perfect man. In his twenty years in the force he had not always acted honourably. His wife had expensive tastes and frequently chastised him for not 'doing what's best for his family.' As far as she was concerned, he was stupid for not throwing in his lot with the Triads. Despite his nagging wife, he'd resisted Charlie's approaches to go 'on the payroll' but he'd occasionally turned a blind eye or done a favour. The demands of his wife were difficult to resist.

He'd told her about his meeting with General Calunsac and his promotion. She was pleased that his social status (and therefore hers) was now improved. But if he wanted to keep this job, and maybe more, he would have to come to some sort of compromise with the new man, Michael. He had no alternative.

"Well thank you for being so forthright, Michael. I understand your position. Life has been difficult lately, Charlie made Angeles impossible to police, I'm glad he's gone. It's a good thing you're here. I'm sure you and I will have a much better working relationship." Michael lightened up now.

"Glad you're happy, son."

He took a sip of his coffee and allowed the tone of the meeting to change.

"Charlie's father has been a best friend for years, and I've known Charlie since he was a baby.

He's always been a problem child, and, between you and me, Xi has indulged him far too much over the years. I hope a spell in Manila under his father's wing will straighten him out, but I'm not so sure."

Protacio nodded and called for more coffee. Michael continued.

"Look, son. You are very shorthanded here, and I don't mind telling you that I have fewer men here than I would like, so it will pay us both to keep things on an even keel, rocking the boat would not help either of us." The captain nodded in agreement.

"There are many ways we can work together, to make life easier, and I want to make you an offer. Our expenses here are much lower now we are not paying out your predecessor, or many of your officers. We are, shall we say, 'cash rich,' In the past you have tried to tread an honourable path, but now that you can see a more mature and sensible 'management' is in place here, you may feel able to work more closely with us."

He reached into a pocket and put a bundle of notes in a rubber band down onto the table Protacio's eyes widened, he hadn't expected such a bold approach, or so soon. He quickly strode over to his office door and locked it. Michael continued.

"There's a million pesos there, son. Call it a welcome gift; and there will be a hundred thousand pesos each month. I know that is going to make your wife happy. It is twice as much as your police salary."

Michael wanted the man to know he'd done his research. Protacio stared at the bundle on the desk; he was uncomfortable about it sitting there, but he didn't want to touch it, yet.

"Well, let's suppose for a minute I could work 'more closely' with you – what would you expect of me?"

Let me make this easier for you, son. I think you already know that you and I can work together better than you could ever work with that brat child. We, the 'family,' have always fared best when we've worked behind the scenes, keeping a low profile. That's the way we'll be doing business from now on – we won't cause you any problems, if you don't cause us any. Are you able to work with that?"

Protacio sipped his refreshed coffee and considered the older man's proposals.

"You make it sound easy, Michael.

Basically, you just want me to let you carry on business as usual? It seems too simple."

"It is simple, son. Maybe, occasionally, we'll want you to use your influence in our favour, and we'd expect your officers to leave our 'operations' alone. I'm sure it's nothing you would find too difficult."

Protacio knew he really didn't have a choice. If he refused, he would not last long in his new post, and then he'd probably lose his marriage. He reached across the table and picked up the money, sliding it into his open desk drawer. Michael smiled.

"Welcome to the team, son." The captain forced a smile. Michael rose to leave.

"Hold on a moment, Michael, there is one thing I need to discuss with you." Michael sat back down.

"All the recent problems have been caused by a dispute over the hotel down the street, the Blue Room Hotel. I think you're aware of the issues. The owner is back in town now, and he wants to meet you."

"That's good news, son. Yes, I want to meet him as well. We certainly have unfinished business. I'll call in today to welcome him back."

***

It was mid-morning; the street was getting busy and hot now. Food vendors were setting up their stalls ready for the lunch trade and smells of barbecued chicken and fish balls filled the air. It was good to walk along the pavement and see people about their ordinary business again.

Today Paul sat at an outside table and watched with approval as the sign writer and his son put the shiny fresh sign above the hotel. Painted in blue and white on the wooden boards, the sign proudly proclaimed 'Parris Island Hotel.'

As the sign was being erected two white guys walked past and looked up.

"Hey, man. Is this place named after the marine training base back home? I spent six months there."

Paul was pleased. That was just the reaction he expected from the ex-pat vets.

"So did I friend, come on in and have a beer."

The police station too had a fresh feel about it. Paul didn't recognize any of the men manning the reception desk, and there did not seem many of them around. Captain Protacio was talking to a junior officer in the corner by the door. He saw Paul and came over.

"It's good to see you back, I told you everything would be different when you returned, Paul. How are things at the hotel?"

The two men shook hands warmly, and the senior officer led Paul down the hall.

"As you can see, everything is quiet now. We're down on manpower, but it's all controllable. It's like a breath of fresh air now that we don't have that hothead Charlie to deal with."

"So, what's this new guy, Michael, like to work with?"

"I think you'll be surprised. He's tough, but he's not your normal thug. He's cultured and educated – with a reputation for fairness. He's Xi's righthand man, so I don't think you'll have any trouble. He said he will call on you later today."

"What about all their illegal businesses, the brothels, the extortion, the drugs?" enquired Paul. Protacio pondered his response.

"Paul, we've just got over one big problem, we have to take matters slowly. There are some things we just have to accept,

I'm afraid. Even if we had the manpower and the political will to clear them out of Angeles entirely, they'd just send more people. Please remember, we are dealing with a worldwide organization, it's not that easy."

"I suppose you're right." Said Paul, grudgingly, as he got up to leave. As he was by the door, he remembered something.

"By the way, what happened to your predecessor, Alvarez? Is he still here?" The captain smiled.

"That man has been transferred to Manila. The charges against him are stacking up – I doubt he'll ever be a free man again."

"Well. It seems you have everything under control now. I'll get back to the hotel. You know where I am if you need me."

The officer came over and put a hand on Paul's shoulder.

"Paul, we've been very grateful for all the help you and your friends have given us over this tough time, but you will have to leave things up to us now."

By the time Paul got back to the inn, the sign was proudly announcing the new name of the hotel. The sign writer had gone. Linda and the staff were outside admiring the shiny sign.

"I like it." Proclaimed Linda.

Other staff nodded and disappeared into the hotel as customers began to come in for lunch'

Jollibee was busy as usual, but they found a space close to the front door. Luckily, his captors had not thought to take his phone a way. While they were parking, Charlie tapped out a message without them seeing.

"I'm here." said the text. Charlie managed to send it, though his battery was very low. He could only hope that they would come and rescue him in time. Once they were back on the road, there would be little opportunity for him to escape.

The three men had a table in the middle with no other customers close.

Through the panoramic window Charlie could see the cars arriving. After a couple of minutes, he saw what he was waiting for. The familiar sleek black SUV drifted around to the back of the building and parked up behind the toilet.

"I need the John," said Charlie.

They could see the door to the toilet from their table.

"I'll go and check it out. Make sure there's no way to escape at the back."

He was gone for less than a minute.

"It's ok. There's a window there, but it's too high for him to reach. It'll be ok."

Charlie stood and ambled through the quiet restaurant and into the toilet. Once secure inside, he looked around. The skylight above the toilet was small, but he thought he could probably squeeze through it; it was set about ten feet above the floor, way above his reach. He texted again.

"I'm in the toilets – one of you come in – just act naturally but get here quickly."

Charlie knew if he took too long, his captors would get suspicious and come to check on him. His two captors were quite relaxed. It was a large Jollibee, so the toilets were spacious, and busy. Several people came and went whilst Charlie was inside. Luckily, when Tony came in there was no one else there.

"Quickly. Sit down and let me stand on your shoulders. I think I can reach that window and get out."

He carefully climbed up the man and stood unsteadily on his broad shoulders. Pain shot through his leg, but getting out was his priority. He could easily reach up and undo the latch from this position, but he couldn't get high enough to ease through the window.

The bandage was turning red – he'd opened up his wound again.

The other man sitting in the car outside noticed the window open and rushed over to it, in case he could help his boss.

"Try to stand up," said Charlie, still standing on the other man's shoulders. With difficulty, the man below him slowly pushed himself up.

"That's it. Nearly there." Charlie called down breathlessly. The pain in his leg was intense, but he had to work through it.

As he stood on the grass below the window, the second man saw his boss's hands appear through the opening. Charlie eased his body through the opening until he was balanced, half in and half out.

He reached down and just touched the fingers of the man below.

"Pull me through, quickly."

The man jumped up and caught hold of the boss's wrists.

"Okay, now pull, but gently." Charlie's body slowly emerged through the aperture and finally fell through and onto the ground. As he got into the car Tony appeared around the side of the building. Charlie wound down the window.

"Quick, get away – they'll soon see I'm not there. We need to be away from here before then."

"He's taking a long time. I'd better go and check." Xi's man went back to the toilet. As he entered, he could see that there was no one there, but he noticed the open window above him. He rushed back.

"He's gone. I'm not sure how, but he got through the window. There's no one there." His startled colleague jumped up.

"Quick, let's search around. He can't have got far."

The two men rushed outside and split up to search the area quicker, but there was no sign of their charge. Out of breath, the two men met up by the entrance.

"What are we gonna tell the boss? He will be mad."

Charlie and his colleagues laughed as they drove away, and watched the helpless captors look desperately around.

"Where are we going, boss?"

"Let's get to Maxwell's house. His wife, Maria is a nurse."

As the car pulled away, Charlie noted the line of fresh red blood leading from the wall to the car.

***

Michael had a relaxed lunch and wandered down to the Parris Island Hotel at around three p.m. He needed the mid-day rush to be over, so he'd have Paul's full attention. He paused at the entrance to look at the new sign with approval. It was very smart. It improved the place.

He needn't have worried about it being busy. The old soldier sat on his own in his usual corner with a coffee; apart from Paul the place was deserted. He rose as the old Chinaman came towards him. Wanting to set the right tone, Michael approached Paul with a wide smile and an outstretched hand. Paul responded warily.

"Hello Paul. I'm Michael, from the Casino down the road. I thought we might have a chat. May I join you?"

Paul glanced over to Linda at the counter to bring over some coffee.

"Well, I know who you are, Michael. Welcome to Angeles. I hope you will enjoy your time here, and I hope we won't have any trouble now we have an adult in charge," Michael smiled.

"Nicely put. I don't think you need to worry. I've been around a lot longer than Charlie, there isn't much I haven't seen, or handled. I think if we both stick to our own 'interests' we'll be fine."

Paul took that as a warning not to take against Michael, or the triads, and the smuggling, prostitution, gambling, etc. He nodded.

"I came here for an easy life, Michael, not to clean up the entire town, but don't misunderstand me. If I need to get involved to protect me and mine, I will. I hope you understand me."

"I do; and I think you've already proved that. You won't need to worry."

Paul sat back and studied Michael. He seemed sincere, perhaps the future did not seem so bad.

"How is Charlie? I have a hunch he will get into trouble wherever he is."

"Well, he should do ok in Manila under his father's wing. He has to keep his nose clean now. We won't see him around here for a couple of years or so."

Paul raised his eyebrows.

"I think his father will be sensible enough to make sure he never shows his face in Angeles again. If he did, I can't guarantee his safety. The veterans have a lot of time on their hands, and they do not forget."

"Well, it's a long time off, and it may never happen. Anyway, I'll be here for the foreseeable future. I like the town."

Michael was keen to bring the conversation back to a friendlier footing. Paul simmered down a bit and let it drop.

"How about you, Paul? How long will you stay here? Is this where you want to spend the rest of your days?"

Paul reflected for a moment.

"Oh, I'm sure there are worse places, but you never know. You can't always control your own future."

"That's very profound, Paul. You can be deep. I guess we'll get along. But before I go, I hope you won't mind me saying that if and when you wanted to move on, we're still interested, and everything will be very fair and open, but no pressure this time."

"I'll bear that in mind." Replied Paul. *I'll burn this place down myself before I'll let you or any of your goons get their hands on it.* Paul thought to himself. He stood and watched Michael disappear out of the door with mixed feelings. He was uncomfortable that Michael had left the door open to Charlie coming back, but on the plus side, he seemed a reasonable guy.

Michael smiled smugly as he walked back down the street. He'd achieved part one - Get on a good footing with Paul - Part two was next. Make Paul want to sell.

***

Next morning Paul came down at his usual time. From across the room he saw a white envelope on his table. It arrived with the post earlier and the staff put on the table where he always sat for breakfast. It bore a foreign stamp. He was pretty sure what it was. His wife's lawyers had traced him to the hotel and were now serving the divorce papers on him again. He put them to one side, but he would read them later, perhaps it was time.

His previous life seemed a lifetime away; but life without her seemed more bearable now. He needed advice. Paul was not good at these sorts of things. He had no-one to talk to, except...

As he absent-mindedly sipped his coffee, Linda came over with his breakfast.

"Look love, there's something I want to talk to you about. Can we have a quiet coffee together when the breakfast service is over?"

"Sure, Paul. Happy to help."

She smiled, then disappeared off to attend to her duties, wondering what her boss might want. Breakfasts were over after an hour and she came back to his table.

"How can I help, Paul?"

"I'm not sure you can, love, but it would be nice just to share my situation with someone, if you don't mind."

"No, that's fine. I'm a sympathetic listener."

She put an arm on his shoulder, then reached over to get them two fresh coffees. For the next hour Paul told her how his wife, Editha, had left him and taken their son abroad, but now she was pushing for a divorce. He showed Linda the papers. She considered for a moment.

"Paul, you've got to fill them in. Nothing's lost. It will be the start of your new life. That's what I guess."

"Thanks for that, Linda."

Paul put the petition back in the envelope.

"You're right. It's time now."

***

In her room, Linda was making an important phone call.

"Hello, Charlie. It's me, can you talk?"

"Hello sweetheart. I'm with Alex now, my dad wanted me to go back to Manila, but I'm not going back there. I got away when we stopped at Jolibee. How are things, I miss you."

"I miss you too. so much. When can I see you?"

Charlie was quiet, but eventually spoke.

"Soon, sweetheart, soon. I've got some things to sort out. I'll ring you soon. This is not over yet. He can't get rid of me that easily."

"Wait, are you still considering getting the hotel? How can you after all that's happened?" Charlie became serious.

"Listen to me sweetheart. You must keep this to yourself. Promise me that. Nobody can know, but I am planning to come back. Swear you won't tell anyone, please, but I'll be there, sooner than you expect, and we can be together." Linda squealed in delight.

"Really, Charlie? I can't believe it. I'd given up hope, sweetheart."

Charlie was reflecting.

"Look, sweetheart. I will need your help to make this work."

"You know I'll do anything for you, Charlie, but what can I do?"

"I'll contact you again in a few days; keep your eyes and ears open."

***

Linda made sure that there was no one around as she took out her phone and dialled.

"He rang me earlier, sir. I felt you should know."

Linda was conflicted. Charlie had acted so strangely, and done some really terrible things of late, but she did not like going behind his back to his father. Perhaps his dad would help him get back on the right track.

"Thanks for telling me, love. Did he say where he was?"

"No, he didn't. He said he'd ring again soon."

"Okay, just call me again after he rings you, we both have his best interests at heart. How are you bearing up with all these things happening?"

"I'll be okay, sir. I'm sure things will settle down soon. Charlie has said he'd marry me when all of this was over. I hope you'll come to the wedding."

Xi was quiet for a few seconds, then he replied.

"Linda, you do realize that he's already married, don't you? He never sees his wife, but he sends her money, I don't expect he's even spoken to her about a divorce. It would take years before he's free to marry."

Linda did not accept what she was hearing. The bombshell hit her with such a force that she nearly collapsed. She sat on the bed to steady herself.

"Why would he do that, sir? Why would he say he would marry me if he's not free?"

"I expect he didn't like to tell you the truth, love. I guess he was worried he might lose you. Look on the bright side; he looks after you doesn't he? Isn't that enough?"

Obviously. Charlie and his father assumed she was just some street whore who'd be grateful for scraps in return for sex. All she'd ever wanted in life was a happy marriage, kids, the usual things. The things Charlie had promised to give her. It was a lie; it was all a lie.

She composed herself. She still had enough wits about her to realize it would not be wise to upset Xi.

"I'm sorry, sir. I'm sure everything will be fine. It just came as a shock, but I'll be happy with what I've got. What will happen with Charlie?"

"He's being idiotic. Instead of coming up here with me, he's run off somewhere. I don't know where he is or what he's planning. But we both know how unreasonable he can be. We've got to find him before he does something we can't protect him from. Do you understand?"

"Yes, sir, I do, and you can count on me." "Thank you, dear." The line clicked off. Xi sat back in his chair and poured a whisky. So, Linda did not realize Charlie was married, and she didn't seem very happy about it. Xi had grown to like her, a lot. If she left the lad it would make managing Charlie more difficult, but there wasn't much he could do about that. He made a mental note to send her a bonus.

Linda was also reflecting. She'd gone along with some awful things, she'd even killed, and that poor kitchen lad had done nothing to deserve it. Linda hardly recognized the girl she'd become. Her family were decent people. They assumed she was earning an honest living and leading a healthy life in the big city. They would be so ashamed if they knew the truth.

She'd had enough now. Charlie had lied to her about the wedding; that was the final straw. Her dreams, her hopes, were shattered. Anger began to replace the shock she'd initially felt.

***

Paul was down early for dinner that evening. Linda brought over his usual drink. He looked up from his newspaper.

"Hello, love. Come and sit with me for a while. The place is quiet."

Linda smiled and sat down. Paul spoke first.

"Thanks for listening to me earlier. It helped me a lot."

"It's a pleasure, Paul. Glad to help. You're a nice guy – I don't like to see you hurt."

Paul didn't notice that she was a little quieter than usual.

It was Paul's habit to go up to his room when most of the customers had left. Tonight was no exception. As he passed Linda's room, there was a quiet sound, he paused. There it was again. There could be no doubt, Linda was crying. Paul waited a short time then knocked gently. There was movement. Linda came to the door and cracked it open, she was hiding her face, but her eyes were puffy.

"What's wrong, love. Are you ok?

"I'm fine, Paul. Thank you for your concern. I'm just being a silly girl. Don't mind me, I'll be okay tomorrow."

She moved as if to close the door, but Paul prevented her from shutting it.

"I've never known you to cry before, love. It must be something serious. Can't you tell me? I might be able to help."

Still sobbing, she moved away from the door allowing Paul to enter. Even though the light was off Paul realized she'd been in bed; she was only wearing a thin gown, but she didn't seem to mind him being there. She was probably preoccupied with her problem. Paul moved toward the light switch.

"Oh no, please don't turn the light on I look awful, I don't want you to see me like this."

Paul sat on the edge of the bed. There were only two chairs in the room; they were both piled high with clothes. She moved over and sat down next to him, trying to control her sobs. Something must have really upset her, figured Paul.

"Come on, love. Tell me what the problem is. I'm sure I can help." This only caused her to sob again. Instinctively he put his arm around her shoulder, she responded by leaning in and resting her head on his chest.

"I'm sorry, Paul. Something's just upset me today. I'll be fine tomorrow. I got some bad news from America – that's all."

It was the first thing she could think of.

"Things sometimes seem worse than they really are, tell me what it's all about love. It'll help you to share it," She quietly nodded.

Linda made up a story to stop Paul's enquiries.

"It's my husband. He's in the U.S. When he married me he promised he'd take me there. We only got married six months ago." "Yes, I heard that love. What's the problem? Is he okay?"

"He's more than ok, Paul. He's got another woman." Paul sighed.

"Oh, I'm sorry to hear that sweetheart. It's probably because he's lonely. Perhaps he'll be different when you are together, things will be fine then." Linda shook her head.

"No, you don't understand. He had to tell me about her because she's pregnant, and he's decided he wants to marry her – he's sending me divorce papers."

"I am sorry to hear that, Linda. I can understand now. How can I help? Do you need some time off? Why don't you go to see your parents?"

Linda cried harder.

"My parents are poor farmers in the Visayas, I wouldn't trouble them with this. I have a brother, but he's in Italy – I'll call him tomorrow. I haven't seen him for six years."

"You should visit your husband in the US, the change will do you good, you can take some time off."

"Thank you, Paul, but I can't. I haven't got the money for the air fare."

"Don't worry, love. I'll pay for your ticket; you don't need to worry."

"Oh, Paul. You're so kind to me." She snuggled closer into him.

It felt nice to be close to Paul. She felt secure, a feeling she'd lost over the last few weeks.

He pulled her closer in what he meant as a fatherly gesture, but Linda thought otherwise. She lifted her head to stare into his eyes. He could see her eyes were still watery, but she was no longer crying. With her eyes closed, she brought her open mouth to his and kissed him passionately.

"Hold on, sweetheart. It would be easy for me to take advantage of you now. I don't want to do that – you're worth more than that."

They kissed again, then just lay in each other arms. After a couple of hours, they fell asleep.

Paul woke as the sun rose, it was six-fifteen a.m. He extricated himself from her arms, kissed her shoulder and left for his own room to shower and change. That was unexpected, but amazing. She obviously really cared. Perhaps this could go somewhere.

He sat down to breakfast about an hour later; she was nowhere to be seen. This was unusual, but Paul was not surprised she was late today. She finally descended the stairs ten minutes later. She looked a little shy, but she came and sat beside him.

"I hope you're better today, love. Let's talk some more later."

"I am, Paul, thanks to you. You are a wonderful person. I can't thank you enough."

She looked around to make sure no-one was looking, then kissed him on the cheek. Paul was getting close to her now, he'd never looked at her that way before because everyone believed she was married and, unusually, faithful. Everything had changed now. He found his mind wandering off into exciting and comforting possibilities. Underneath the table she gently squeezed his knee.

"You're so kind, Paul. I hope we'll do more than talk." Paul was happy but surprised. So last night may not just be a one-off after all.

"No need to get me a ticket, Paul. I've decided not to go. He's not worth it. I'll sign the divorce papers when he sends them."

CHAPTER

NINE

Charlie Recovers

Maxwell feared his wife would not be happy, but he had to tell her.

"Can you get the spare room ready, sweetheart? We've got a friend coming to stay."

"Okay, sweetheart, that's nice, who is it?"

Maria swept past him into the kitchen with plates in her hands.

"It's Charlie. He needs somewhere to rest up for a while."

Maria ambled back through with a face like thunder.

"Why the hell did you invite him here? He's a murderer. I hoped we'd heard the last of him. I don't want him here."

Maxwell expected she'd react like this.

"Maria, I'm sorry, they didn't give me a choice. They said they've got to come here because you're a nurse. Charlie's been shot in the leg – he's bleeding."

"My God, you realize he's been replaced here, don't you? He's not in charge of the drug dealers now. Someone in the market told me it's an older guy. They say Charlie ran away. We can't get involved in any gang war, Maxwell – we've got young children."

"They'd be in more danger if I'd refused him, love. He can be vicious if he's displeased."

"I suppose so. Who else is coming – you said 'they'?"

"Tony is with him, and one more guy. But they're not staying. They're just helping him secretly – his father, Xi, doesn't realize."

As Maxwell finished the black car pulled up outside.

"Oh my God, they're here. I'll put extra sheets on the bed – I must treat him there."

As Maria rushed away there was a knock on the door.

Maxwell opened it and Tony pushed through, supporting Charlie.

"Bring him through here," Maria called from the bedroom.

Charlie was pale now and winced every time he had to put his foot down. With Tony's help he limped through and shouted with pain as they helped him to lie out on the bed. The bandage around his leg was deep red and glistening with fresh blood.

Maria noticed the trail of droplets leading back to the front door. She'd rather be mopping them up than helping this crook.

"Have you got anything for the pain?"

Charlie's voice was weak. Maria went to the bathroom and came back with two pills and a glass of water.

"These will help."

She helped him sit up to sip the water. She only had sleeping pills in the house, but she figured they may take the edge off and at least keep him a little quiet.

Maria waited for twenty minutes until she saw his eyes drooping. She didn't want to wait any longer to deal with that leg. It was still oozing blood.

She unwound the bandage, lifting his leg gingerly when she had to. Before she took off the final wrap, she prepared a bowl of hot water and fresh bandages by the bed. As the last piece of lint came away from the leg, it stuck to the wound. Rather than yank it off, Maria wiped around the wound with a clean cloth and the water. It still caused Charlie discomfort, but with the pills and his weakened state all he could do was to moan.

Finally, she could see what she was dealing with. The jagged hole was red and angry, and puffy at the edges. She lifted the leg and saw that the exit wound looked the same. There was only a little blood oozing out now, but the bright redness told her there was an inflammation - the leg was infected. As Maria poured iodine onto a clean cloth she turned to Tony and Maxwell.

"This will be painful. Hold his shoulder down – he'll probably shout, but he needs this – we've got to stop the infection. I only have iodine here, but I'll bring home some antibiotics when I finish at the hospital."

As the iodine-soaked cloth wiped around the holes, Charlie tried to scream, but little sound came out. He was weaker than he looked.

Oh my God, thought Maria. What if he dies? What will these guys do? An enormous part of her wished he would die but feared the consequences. She'd have to try her best to keep him alive.

The angry wounds concerned the trained nurse. He needed strong antibiotics, but there was no way she could get them until she smuggled them out of the hospital at the end of her shift.

Once she'd finished, and with the pills taking full effect Charlie drifted away to sleep.

Tony looked down at the shallow breathing body and spoke to Maria.

"Will he be okay?" said Tony.

"His infection needs treating, but I think he'll be fine. He'll need a couple of days rest before he can move though."

Tony frowned.

"Remember who his father is. They might have fallen out, but I wouldn't want to be the one to explain to Xi Wong that I let his son die," Tony and the other man moved towards the door. We've got to get back to the office before they wonder where we are. Michael does not know we're helping Charlie. We'll return tonight. Take good care of him, love."

They shut the door behind themselves as they left. Maria pulled Maxwell into the kitchen.

"I want that man out of here as soon as possible. I knew that working for him would bring us trouble."

She started to put her coat on.

"You must look after him while I'm away. I doubt he'll come round, and I'll be back in eight hours. If I can get away earlier, I will."

She flounced out the door before Maxwell could respond.

***

In Manila, the phone rang in Xi's office.

"I don't know what you're doing, Michael, but whatever it is, carry on doing it." Xi smiled.

Profits from the casino had increased by fifty percent since the new man took over.

"We're seeing an increase in every area – and our expenses are lower – you're managing it with fewer men."

"Yes, things have quietened down, and everything is running smoothly. I'll stay another month or two and then come back. I think we can safely leave Tony and Alex to run this show. He's firm, but he doesn't take risks. That's what we need now. I must tend to my activities in Manila, it doesn't do to be away too long."

"Sure, I understand that. I'll leave that up to you. I don't think anything will go wrong in Angeles now, but I will send four more of my men down there before you come away. We have no idea where Charlie is. I hope he's gone far away, but we can't be sure. I'd like some of my guys around there, just in case."

"That's fine by me."

Xi needed to say something to Michael but was not sure the right way to put it.

"Just one thing, my friend. Why do you think profits have increased so much since you took over?"

Michael was equally hesitant to respond, but he had to.

"Xi, my old friend. I think you know the answer. Charlie was taking a large share of the money and keeping it for himself – I can't see any other explanation."

"Don't worry, Michael. I'd worked that out for myself. You are so lucky you have a son you can be proud of. I despair to think what will become of my lad, if he ever shows up again."

"Oh, I'm sure you'll hear from him. He'll get into some trouble and need you again. The question is, what will you do with him? Over the years he's probably stashed away a fortune, I wonder what he's done with it?"

"Well, he won't have put it in a bank – we'd have found out about that. I'm sure he's hidden it well somewhere."

"I guess we must sort that out when we find him."

"One last thing, what are we going to do about that hotel, are we still interested in it."

"I met with Paul, the owner. He's a reasonable guy, but he doesn't want to sell, and he'd cause a lot of problems if we tried to force him. I think we've got more important things right now. We'll look at it again later."

Xi said goodbye to his friend and wished him well. Michael put the phone down. He was sorry for his old friend. Charlie had always been difficult, but lately he'd really gone off the rails. Michael thought he needed psychiatric help, but he'd probably never accept it.

***

Maria left her job early. By four p.m. she walked through the gate of the hospital with a five-day supply of antibiotics hidden in her purse. When she got home, she found Charlie talking to

Maxwell. Charlie was still laying on the bed but seemed a little stronger.

"Thank God you're back. I need more painkillers."

He winced as he tried to move. Marie brought two more white pills and some water. She fished in her bag and found the antibiotic and gave him two blue pills as well, which he swallowed without question. Lifting his leg carefully, she inspected the dressing. There was no blood so maybe it didn't need changing tonight – she'd check it in the morning.

"Has he eaten anything?" Maria enquired as she put the kettle on for coffee.

"I found some chicken soup and gave him some at lunchtime. He ate a little."

"Well it's good he's got an appetite, I suppose. I'll fix him something else later."

"Maria!" Charlie called from the bedroom.

"That coffee smells wonderful. Can I get some?"

"I'm glad you're feeling better." Maria called back.

As she walked through to him with a coffee, she heard a shout and found him trying to get out of bed. He winced with pain as his foot touched the floor.

"Charlie? What are you doing? You'll open up the wound again. Don't put any weight on it yet, maybe tomorrow, but you've got to take it easy. Get that leg back on the bed. I'll redo the dressings now."

Maria carefully peeled and unwound the dressing, which was thankfully still white, until she got down to the wound. It was still red, but no worse than last night. That was the best that Charlie could hope for.

"I'll give you more pills before you sleep, but you must keep your weight off it. Give it a rest at least for tomorrow – maybe the day after you can try to put some weight on it."

"When will I be able to drive? I need to go somewhere."

Maria was conflicted between her instinct as a nurse to care for an injured man and her need to get him out of the house as quickly as possible.

"If you open those wounds again, you're going to be in serious trouble, Charlie. Provided you rest properly you can walk around a bit the day after tomorrow. If everything's okay then, you can drive in four or five days."

At that moment the front door opened; Tony walked in, without knocking. He strode straight into the bedroom just as Maria was coming out. He was pleased to see his boss sitting up in bed.

"Tony. What's the news? What is Michael doing?"

"There's not much change, boss. He spends a lot of time talking to your dad."

Charlie knew it would not be long before they discovered that a lot of money had gone missing. His way forward was clear, and he'd have to start the plan as soon as possible.

"It's best you don't come here again, Tony; at least, not for a while. We must make sure no one looks for me here. Stay away for two days, then come round with a car. I will be able to drive by then. Bring a new SUV – I have a lengthy drive. I'll be going on my own."

Xi was having a hard day. The boy had been a problem since he was young - always in trouble and taking no notice of anyone. He was Xi Wong's son and could do what he liked. Charlie's mother died of breast cancer when he was ten. Xi was distraught, but Charlie showed very little emotion; he spent little time with his mother in her dying days, and seemed to forget the event quickly. For Xi however, it took him years to recover from his wife's death – if he ever did.

He'd promised his wife he'd take care of Charlie, no matter what. The lad's behavior made that promise increasingly difficult.

It wasn't often that Xi didn't know what he should do, but now was one of those times. He'd rescued the boy from a dangerous situation the lad had created in Angeles, and the boy thanks him by running off, probably with the millions of dollars he'd stolen over the years. Xi wanted him back in Manila, but he was not sure he could control him. Charlie was getting stronger, while Xi was getting weaker with age.

***

Paul had a smile like a Cheshire cat when he sat down with Linda at the end of the dinner service. From behind his back he brought a bottle of champagne. He theatrically pulled out the cork with a 'pop.'

"What's the occasion, Paul? Are we celebrating?"

"Yes, we are, love. I have signed my divorce papers and sent them back today. I'll concentrate on the future now, not the past." Linda smiled.

"That's great news, Paul. Let's do this properly then."

She went to the bar and returned with champagne glasses which Paul filled.

"Here's to your future, Paul."

She raised her glass high in the air. Paul smiled and lifted his glass to link with hers, their eyes met for a lingering moment.

"How about 'here's to OUR future'" Paul said, Linda giggled.

"Yes, that's better – I guess we both have some big changes to go through now, but positive ones." They chinked glasses again.

"Have you had any divorce papers from your husband in America yet? inquired Paul.

Linda was quiet. She'd have to tell him the truth sometime, now was as good a time as any, she thought.

"Paul, I hope you won't hold it against me, but there is no American husband. I'm not married. I spread that around so I wouldn't get hit on all the time, and I was crying before for a family reason I didn't want to discuss. I'm sorry Paul; I hope you understand."

Paul smiled, "It's fine, love, I quite understand, and I don't blame you. It was a sensible thing to do. I'm realizing what a thoughtful and honourable girl you are."

He reached over and held her hand. She squeezed his hand and smiled.

He rose, still holding her hand and raised her up into his arms. *He kisses very well,* thought Linda as she returned his embrace. They broke their kiss only to climb the stairs. Linda wanted this. The anger was still within her. Charlie couldn't marry her. He never had any intention of marrying her, but she'd have to be careful how she dealt with the situation. Charlie would be angry and vindictive if she spurned him. She'd have to think of a way. She felt safe with Paul, but she'd be discreet for a while.

Light streaming through the window heralded the morning. Paul sat up in the bed, his eyes squinting as Linda threw back the covers. He looked at the watch on his bedside table. Six a.m.

"Do you need to get up so early, love?" Linda laughed.

"Rise and shine, sleepyhead. I've got to start breakfasts. You stay there and have a rest."

Paul lay back down as she shut the door behind her. An hour later he rose and followed her downstairs. She brought him over his coffee as usual, but he grabbed her hand before she could walk away. She giggled as he pulled her to him.

"Not now, Paul. It's better that the staff don't know yet. Let's take it slowly. Is that ok?"

Paul released her hand.

"Whatever you want, sweetheart. We have all the time in the world."

***

The call she dreaded came late afternoon; she was resting after a busy lunch session. Linda hoped he wouldn't contact her today; she still had to think about how to deal with the situation. She couldn't ignore the incessantly ringing phone; Charlie might just turn up looking for her. He was very unpredictable, and she didn't want Paul to find out about Charlie if possible.

"Keep this to yourself, sweetheart. I've got to be very careful, but I'm staying at Maxwell's place. They shot me in the leg, but Maxwell's wife, Maria is looking after me, my leg is nearly fixed. I'll be up and about tomorrow. Come over tonight, I have some news."

"Okay, I can get away for a couple of hours, but I must be back in time for dinners. I'll be with you in half an hour."

Linda usually went to the market at this time, so Paul never questioned her when she left.

The walk to Maxwell's house took her just twenty minutes. Maria saw her coming through the window and opened the door before she knocked.

"Keep quiet, Linda. He drifted off to sleep after he called you. We'll let him doze for a while. Come into the kitchen, we can talk."

Linda sat on a tall stool and accepted the coffee offered by Maria who closed the door in case Charlie woke. She didn't want him to overhear her conversation with Linda.

The two girls embraced. They'd been friends since school, but these days they didn't see much of each other. Maria spoke quietly, the fear showed on her face.

"I'm glad to you're here, Linda. I realize he's your boyfriend but I'm afraid of him. I hate having him in the house. I can sense his eyes undressing me as I walk around. He's creepy. I've told Maxwell, but he's too frightened of Charlie to do anything."

"It's ok, Maria, I appreciate what he's like. He's becoming more uncontrollable these days. Did you realize he's fallen out with his father?"

"Yes, I think that's why he ended up here. No one knows he's here. He's hiding out until he is better."

"How is his leg? Did they hurt him badly?"

"Only a flesh wound, but the bullet hit an artery and went straight through. The wound is on the mend, but he seemed weak for a while. He'll be walking tomorrow, and I think he plans to drive the day after."

"Drive? Where to?"

"I've no Idea, Linda, perhaps he'll tell you."

"Maybe he will. Maria, there is some-thing else you should know."

She spoke in hushed tones now.

"I don't want to be with him anymore – I'm trying to work out a way to end the relationship, but I don't think it'll be easy."

"Why? What's happened, Linda? I thought you loved him."

"I do… did. The bastard lied to me. He promised he'd marry me, and then I find out he's already married. I can never be his wife. He just wanted to use me. Charlie doesn't realize I know yet; his father told me. He's shattered my world, Maria.

Everything I thought I could rely on has fallen apart. I hate him Maria; but I must be careful - he could be dangerous."

At that moment, a shout came from the bedroom.

"Maria? Where are you? Where is everybody?"

Charlie woke up in a daze. Maria responded.

"I'm here, Charlie."

The two girls moved through to the bedroom. Charlie smiled, pleased to see Linda, as she followed Maria into the room. Linda approached the bed and held his hand. Maria left them alone and discretely slipped back into the kitchen.

"How are you, Charlie? How's the leg?"

Charlie tried to lift it, but gently let it down as he winced with pain.

"It's better than yesterday, Love. I will try walking around a bit today. I need to be driving tomorrow.'

"You should take it easy. You're not well enough to drive, yet – you'll open the wound. It's your right leg. You'll need to move it a lot. What's so urgent that you can't put it off for a few days?"

"I've got business in Manila, sweetheart. It can't wait, but I won't be long. When I come back, I have just one more thing to do, then we can go away for a fresh start. Would you like that?"

Linda forced a smile and squeezed his hand.

"Of course, I would, sweetheart; that would be great."

She leaned over and kissed his forehead.

"You're looking tired sweetheart, I'll let you rest now. Just let me know you when you get back."

In reality, she couldn't wait to get away.

***

Tony arrived early the next evening. The sleek black car pulled up outside Maxwell's house just after seven a.m. Charlie had been gingerly moving around for an hour. The pain was sharp, but bearable, and his leg felt stronger, if he didn't put weight on it. If he was careful, the wound would not reopen. Maria watched him limp towards the gate, relieved that in a moment he would no longer be her responsibility.

Maybe the wound would heal, perhaps the infection would clear up. She didn't care. She just hoped she'd never set eyes on the nasty hoodlum again.

He drove away without a thank you or any other words to Maria, and Tony strode off in the other direction. Maxwell came out and put his hand on her shoulder, but she shrugged him off.

"I don't want him back here, Maxwell. He is vicious, we both know what he can do, and he gives me the creeps. Can't you keep him away?

"Maria, you know he can be vindictive when he gets upset. There's nothing we can do about it. I'm sorry."

"Well there may be nothing you can do, but I don't have to look at him again. I'm taking the kids to stay with mum for a couple of weeks, maybe then things will be settled, and I can come back."

Maxwell replied to her, but she ignored him. She brushed past and threw an empty case on the bed to pack her bags.

Charlie stopped for a coffee an hour down the road. His leg did not hurt too much, but he wanted to give it a rest. If it got worse today, it would spoil all his plans. He found that if he did everything slowly, he could get by. He sighed with relief; it was comfortable when he had settled in the car seat – he'd adjusted the seat so that the pressure on his foot was light, it was bearable.

He got a corner table and checked his phone. No messages, but he made a call.

"Mr. Johnson? Hello, my name is... Bruce. You have been recommended by a friend. Can I call in to see you this afternoon? I plan to be there around three p.m."

Mr. Johnson agreed. Satisfied, Charlie left the rest of his coffee and started for the door.

He carefully climbed back into the car and set off. He wanted to be in Manila soon after lunch. The gas tank showed full, so unless his wound got worse, he wouldn't need to stop again.

As he approached the city, his leg was aching. He only had two pain pills left, and he wanted to save one for later. He was nearly at his destination now, just another ninety minutes – his timing was good. Time for lunch.

The large Jollibee restaurant seemed busy, but he found a bench where he could lift his leg up to rest it – he was nervous of using more high-class establishments in case someone recognized him. He wouldn't have to hide like this for long.

Charlie chose this restaurant deliberately. Across the road was 'Johnson Realtors.' He had an appointment with Albert Johnson after lunch.

There were many things Charlie had not told his Dad, this business was one of them.

"I require a small warehouse, Mr. Johnson.

It must be in a quiet area and we're happy to take anything run down. We don't need it for prestige. It's a working business, we'll be using it for storage."

"I think we may have just the place for you, Mr....?"

"Just call me Bruce."

Albert Johnson did not push; he could find out all the details later if 'Bruce' wanted to go ahead.

"I can take you there now if you have the time."

"Sure. The sooner the better."

Manila traffic stretched out nose to tail, but within the hour they approached a dreary, run down, trading estate. More than half of the buildings had been abandoned. The unit Mr. Johnson was showing Charlie sat right at the end of the last lane. There were a few broken windows, but the doors looked solid.

"It'll need some doing up, but the cheap rent should make up for that."

"What happened here, Mr. Johnson? Why is the place like a cemetery? We haven't seen another person since we came onto the estate."

"Someone opened a newer, bigger business park just a mile away, but easier to get to from the major roads. They tempted the tenants away with cheap rent deals. I must be honest with you. This place has been derelict for over three years. No-one is interested in it."

"Well, let's see – can you show me around?"

"Sure, follow me. No one has shown any interest in it – so if you're interested it will be very affordable."

Mr. Johnson needed a few minutes to work the old and rusty lock, but soon they walked inside. The windows, brown with grime, were broken, and it took a while for their eyes to adjust to the dim light. It was just a big, dirty, open space Two metal roller doors at the front were dented and rusty; and the only other entrance, a small wooden door around the back with no lock, was bolted from inside.

It didn't take them long to look around, there was nothing to see. Soon the two of them were standing outside again. Mr. Johnson locked up.

"Hang on a minute, I think I've left my car keys in there. I won't be a minute."

Charlie slipped back inside and dashed to the back door. Furtively, he looked over his shoulder to make sure Johnson was not watching, then he drew back the bolt before running to the front and joining Albert.

"It may be ok, but I need to talk it over with some associates before I can decide."

Mr. Johnson nodded sullenly. He'd heard this many times before. Bruce wouldn't be back.

***

Charlie knew his father's habits. Unless he stayed out of town, he would work on until about nine p.m. on his own. Most of his people left around six or seven p.m.

At just after seven the phone rang. Xi sat at his ornate desk relaxing with the first whisky of the evening.

"Dad, is that you?"

Xi recognized his wayward son's voice straightaway.

"Charlie? Nice to hear from you, son. Why did you run away? I wanted to bring you back to Manila for your own good. Where are you? Is everything ok?"

"Dad, I'm in Manila, and I need to see you. I'm sorry; I handled the Angeles situation badly. I let it get to me personally. Dad, I realize how badly I acted, and I want to put it right. Can I come over? I can be there in thirty minutes."

Xi sighed, He'd never been able to trust Charlie. To put him in charge of his own team so far away was a terrible idea. He realized that now, but this 'repentance' seemed too good to be true. Did he really come to make amends? or did he just want more money to get out of some sort of scrape? There was only one way to find out.

"You'd better come to the office, son. I'm still here working. I'll wait for you."

The premises from which Xi Wong ran his vast and powerful business empire was not a large and imposing office block in the centre of the city as you would expect. For over twenty years, he'd run and grown his organization from an old and imposing family house in the Das Marinas suburb of Manila.

He also lived in the office block. In his business personal security was important, and it was easier to protect himself this way.

Since his wife, Charlie's mother, died, Xi lived alone there. He'd given up round-the clock security years ago. Unlike most of the high-profile mobsters in the Philippines, Xi hadn't had any serious threats to his person, or his business for years. This was due to the way he ran things. Everyone learned that if you crossed him, you would suffer. But if you were straight with him, he would treat you fairly.

Instead of the guards in the grounds and on the rooftops that most of his peers maintained, he'd changed over to tall, solid, steel gates and razor wire on the walls. It was impossible to get into the compound unless you were invited or well known to the old man.

Charlie waved his plastic entry card at the small metal box mounted on a post in front of the gates. He was pleased to hear the familiar buzz and watch the heavy motorized barrier begin to move. Thankfully, his entry pass still worked.

He drove through and into the familiar parking area. The front door was already open. It silhouetted the frame of his father against the hall light, the old man had come out to meet his son. He walked out and hugged the boy briefly; Charlie pulled away. Any affection between them was lost a long time ago. Xi guided him through the kitchen and into his office, choosing to sit in a long couch and beckoning his son to sit down beside him."

"I'm surprised to get a warm welcome, Dad. You didn't really want me back. That's why I didn't come with your men."

"No matter what you've done, you're still my son, and I love you. Anyway, what have you done now? I'll help you if I can."

"I've come because I want to put things right in Angeles, Dad. There is unfinished business there for me, and I'm back to finish it."

The old man sighed and moved forward, putting an arm on his son's shoulder.

"Son, you can't go back there. You've got to get this obsession out of your mind. I'd hoped you would learn to be different if you worked with me again for a while; there's nothing in Angeles for you now. I'm sad you're still thinking about Angeles. Even when I can allow you to work on your own again, it won't be in Angeles. You'll stay here in Manila, but you're not ready for that yet, son. I hope you will be one day."

"But, dad. It wasn't just me that was disrespected in Angeles, it was you, and the entire organization. Someone's got to put that right. Can't you see that?"

"Things should never have got that bad there, Charlie. It's your poor decisions that caused us all the problems. I can never let you go back to Angeles. No-one wants you there. Things are quiet now, and our business is picking up again. I'm sorry son, but you obviously haven't learned anything yet."

Xi noticed that his son's face was now red, and his breathing was heavy. He'd seen this before. It happened just before Charlie would have a bout of uncontrollable anger, He would lash out at everyone, often doing damage and harm.

"Come on, son. Calm down. We can make this right if we work together. Don't let it upset you so much." Xi moved towards his drinks cabinet.

"Have a drink with me son. We are family.

We can work something out if we try hard."

Charlie now stood facing away from his dad, Xi could see his hands were shaking as he put them inside his jacket.

Xi came forward and put his arms on his boy's shoulder.

"Come on son, things are not so bad. I'll help you get… ungh…

It felt like a hard punch as Charlie turned into his father and plunged his knife into the man's stomach. After a second, the startled man realized it wasn't a punch as Charlie pulled the knife upwards, cutting through flesh, intestines and up, to slice the lung, before pulling it out. His expert cut would be fatal. He was glad he didn't have to use his gun, it would have been messier, there might have been an exit wound. This was much easier than he thought it would be.

Xi's face whitened as he sank to his knees, wheezing and starting to bring up blood as his lung collapsed.

"Son, why?… How could you…?

Stony-faced, the son watched as the old man toppled to the side. Charlie's face was stony. He felt no remorse.

"You've never supported me, Dad. This is all your fault. If you had loved me, we would have been fine. I'm not to blame for any of this."

He was talking to a dead man now. There was no remorse as he stared down at his father, no regret. He'd stood in the way between Charlie and his future. There was no other solution.

Xi was lying on his back, his shirt was bloody, but there was no trace on the floor, Charlie looked around to make sure before going outside to his car. He backed the heavy car up to the door where minutes ago he'd been welcomed by his dad. He opened the tailgate and dragged the limp body over the drive and lifted it into the open tailgate taking care that no blood was spilled.

Next to Xi's office was a small security center where the six screens showed all movement in and around the building. There were three cameras that had picked up his arrival and his activities. Luckily, he remembered how the system worked. It only took him a few minutes to delete all records of him having been there.

He checked the office, and was careful to leave it as he found it. It would be a real puzzle tomorrow when Xi's people came in. They would wonder where the boss was, but wouldn't be too worried for a while; the old man occasionally disappeared for a day or two on 'business' telling no one. On the way out he dropped the catch on the door so someone would have to unlock it to get in.

He drove carefully, the last thing he needed was to be pulled over, it took him forty-five minutes to reach the deserted trading estate. It was even more eerie and empty at this time of night; there was no street lighting. Once the body was inside, he dragged it to a corner and covered it with a tarpaulin. It did not look out of place with the other rubble and rubbish. With a bit of luck, it would be months before anyone might find it.

Charlie found a cheap hotel nearby. He'd used up the last of his painkillers when he killed his dad and the pain was coming back. He eased himself into the bed. He would have to rest before moving on.

After a late breakfast the next day, he took some paracetamol, bought from a local pharmacy. The pain wasn't too bad, he should be ok. He rose and approached the reception desk to settle the bill and made one more call before limping to the car and setting off.

Time was ticking. He would have to hurry. By his reckoning he had the rest of today and maybe tomorrow before Xi's disappearance would become suspicious. He looked at his watch.

If he set out now, he could be in Angeles by late afternoon.

TEN

—◁•▷—

Charlie Returns

Sam was unlocking the large white front door as usual at eight a.m. She had been with Xi and his organization for eleven years. She had earlier left her career as a banker after the auditors found some discrepancies in her accounts. The bank did not want adverse publicity, so she agreed to leave quietly if they did not press charges.

She followed her everyday routine, and walked through to the kitchen to make a coffee. The kettle was cold. That was unusual. Xi usually had his first drink of the day before she arrived. She took the steaming cup through to Xi's office to find it empty.

Xi occasionally had a late morning after a hectic day, so she wasn't too worried. She'd give him until eleven a.m. and, if he hadn't appeared by then, she'd take him up a coffee.

No one had ever really defined the job she did. Xi took her on after her departure from the bank, mainly because the 'errors' she made were in his favor – he owed her.

She'd proved to be loyal and good at her job. Over the years her influence grew, and she was now de facto manager. There were about ten people who worked through or from the office and they usually started rolling about nine thirty. As the staff started to wander into their offices, the day seemed more normal.

Sam went about her usual daily chores until at eleven a.m. she realized that Xi still had not appeared. It was time for coffee anyway, so she made two cups. One for her and one for Xi then climbed the carpeted stairs to the first floor.

Xi's bedroom was down the corridor on the right. She knocked on the door. "Mr. Xi? It's Sam. I've brought you a coffee." There was no response.

She pushed at the door, not wanting to make a noise, and peered around into the room. The larger ornate bed which Xi had owned for twenty years was empty, and perfectly made. Xi had not slept there last night.

Back in Angeles, in the room above the casino, Michael took his first call of the day. He recognized the Manila number; it was Xi's office.

"Hello, who is this?"

"Michael, this is Sam from Manila, is Xi with you?"

"No Sam, I haven't seen him or heard from him for a while. Is something wrong?"

"We're not sure. He didn't sleep in his bed last night, and there's no sign of him today. We are getting a little worried. It's been a while since he's disappeared like this without telling us.

We've called all the places we can think of. Do you have any idea where he might be?"

Michael had an ominous suspicion; he was still trying to find Charlie. No one knew where he had gone after his escape. He hoped two events weren't related.

"Try not to worry Sam, sometimes he will just disappear for a day or two. I'm sure he'll turn up."

Unofficially, Michael was the second in command for the entire country, so he felt he should take some control.

"Are there any issues that need immediate attention in the office, Sam?"

"I don't think so, Michael. Everything seems to be going fine. What do you want me to do?"

"I think for now we must just wait and see what happens. If he doesn't turn up today, I'll come down tomorrow. For now, just keep me informed; call me whenever you need me. He'll be back soon."

Sam rang off. Michael was worried. He rang Captain Protacio down the road at the police station.

"Have you heard anything from Charlie, Captain? He's gone missing, no one seems to know where he is."

"No, I haven't, not since before they took him to Manila."

"He never got to Manila, Captain. He escaped his escort just outside of Angeles. No one's seen him for over four days. Could you ask around your men? Someone may know something."

"I see. I'll let you know. I'll get my men to ask around. Let's hope he doesn't come back, Michael. The trail of destruction he left will take years to put right."

"You and me both, my friend." Michael met with his men.

"Listen boys. Charlie has disappeared. I think he may head back here. Keep your ears and eyes open."

***

Charlie was about an hour out of Manila when his leg felt a little better. He'd managed to pick up some stronger painkillers at a dispensary outside the metropolis.

There was a little blood seeping through the bandage now. He needed to get it re-dressed.

If he stayed with Maxwell's, it would kill two birds with one stone. He required three stops for coffee and a rest on his way back, his leg really ached now.

As he pulled up at Maxwell's house the younger lad was sat on the porch with a beer in his hand.

"Come and help me. I need to get into the house."

Maxwell jumped to Charlie's command and got to the car just as Charlie opened the door. The gangster carefully lifted his leg out of the car and tried not to put any weight on it. He held onto Maxwell and pulled himself out. With his arm around the younger man's shoulder he limped into the house. Maxwell assisted him through and laid him back on the now familiar bed. Charlie groaned as his leg came to rest on the sheets.

"Where's Maria? This dressing needs changing, and I need some more powerful painkillers."

"Maria's away, Charlie. She's taken the kids to her Mom's for a break."

"Well. You have to do it then. Get some dressings and find out where she keeps those pills."

Maxwell knew better than to argue.

"And make me a coffee."

Charlie shouted after the disappearing Maxwell.

Once Charlie was settled on the bed and had coffee and pills; he calmed a bit.

"Give me thirty minutes for the pills to take effect before you do the bandage."

Maxwell readied the tape and the gauze for when Charlie would be ready. As he prepared the tray he wished Maria was there. He was a weak man and didn't know how to cope with the aggressive mobster. She was not picking up her phone. He left her a text message.

When are you coming back? I need you. I miss the kids x

He didn't tell her that Charlie was there – that would make her stay away longer.

After a while he brought fresh bandages through. And a bowl with hot water – he'd seen Maria do that the first time.

Maxwell lifted Charlie's his leg and began to carefully unwind the bandage. A patch of dark red appeared and got bigger as Maxwell unwound the gauze. It stuck and Charlie glared at him each time he had to pull it away.

"Look. Soak the fucking thing with that warm water. That'll make it easier to unwind."

Maxwell was nervous, his hands shook as he gently loosened the bandage, adding warm water as he went. Charlie would be angry if Maxwell hurt him. Finally, the wrapping was off. The wound did not look angry, but it was still seeping. It looked better than a few days ago. Maxwell cleaned the wound with antiseptic and began to re-dress the leg, a little more confident now. He's watched Maria a few nights ago, so he knew what to do.

Finally, he stepped back and admired his handiwork.

"That's not a bad job, Maxwell. Thanks."

Charlie smiled. It was the first time that Maxwell saw the gangster smile.

"Fetch me some whiskey, I'll take it with my pills. It will help me sleep."

Maxwell left Charlie with a large tumbler – he could see the man was tired now.

Charlie woke with the dawn the next day.

"Maxwell. Bring me some coffee. I must get up soon."

As Maxwell boiled the kettle, he wondered how much longer he'd have to put up with having Charlie there. It was like babysitting a volcano. As if to answer him, Charlie shouted.

"I will need you today. Make sure you're around this afternoon. It'll just be a couple of hours, then I'll drop you back. I won't be staying here tonight."

"That's fine, boss," said Maxwell, glad that they would soon be rid of the man.

"I'm hungry. Pick me up some fried chicken – KFC is just down the street."

"Sure boss, I'll go now."

Charlie's leg still ached, but it was better than yesterday, so his mood was lighter.

About ten a.m. he called Tony.

"Tony. I'm back. Can you come here?"

"Glad you're back Charlie. What do you need me to do? I can do whatever you want today. Michael has gone to Manila. He set off early this morning. He didn't say why."

Charlie knew why, but he wasn't saying – he didn't want Tony putting two and two together.

"Listen, there's something I need you to do today, but I don't want to talk to you about it over the phone. Can you come round to Maxwell's house?'

"Sure, I'll be there soon."

Within the hour Tony appeared at the door holding two Starbucks coffees and rang the doorbell.

Maxwell let him in and followed him through to Charlie who was now sitting upright.

Charlie addressed Maxwell.

"I need to talk with Tony; make yourself scarce for an hour."

Maxwell was pleased to get away and left. There was a bar along the street, and he needed a drink. Tony sat on the bed next to Charlie.

"How's the leg? You're looking a lot better than the last time I saw you."

"Yeah, it's nearly mended now. I'm ready for the next step, and I need you to help me."

"I've always supported you, boss, you know that, but what can we do?"

"Tony, during my time here I've built up quite a stash. There's plenty of cash for us to start over – somewhere fresh. I've always had my eyes on Vigan. It's a long way from Manila so it doesn't get much attention from the big boys, but it's easy to bring supplies in through Pagudpud, and there are more wealthy guys there now. We could clean up. I'll pay you a lot more than Michael does, and we'll build our own team – you'll be second in command – how does that sound?"

"But what about Xi, your dad? He won't like that – he'll send people to find us." Charlie smiled.

"My old man won't be sending anyone after us Tony, he won't be sending anyone anywhere ever again. Dealing with him was the business I had to attend to in Manila. He's dead Tony, that's why Michael had to run off to Manila so quickly this morning."

Tony realized Charlie hated his father, but he was surprised the man had gone this far. This development made a difference. Michael would have more power and did not like Tony, who he knew to be Charlie's friend. For Tony, now would be a good time to disappear. If he left, there would be no going back. Michael might suspect he'd been involved in Xi's death; things were becoming too uncertain, too dangerous here. He must get away.

"In that case, I'm all in. What do you want me to do?"

"I've got one piece of unfinished business here before we go. Come back later – I'll call you when. Find some dynamite – a couple of sticks will do. I can't let Paul get one over on me with the hotel. I have to finish him before I go. That's what I need the explosives for. I'm going to blow up Parris Island Hotel. We'll be a long way away from here before anyone puts two and two together. If my reputation follows me, it will be for dealing with enemies, not for giving in. People will be wary before they mess with me. As soon as I've sorted that out, we can be away. Oh, and give me your knife. I left mine in Manila."

As soon as Tony left, Charlie stood, carefully. He gradually put weight on his injured leg and sighed with relief - it didn't hurt too much. He shuffled around the room and then rested. After a couple for minutes he heard Maxwell return.

"Give me some painkillers please. We have to go out."

Maxwell didn't question the man. Charlie walked out to his car unaided, but still limped. Maxwell climbed into the passenger seat, afraid to ask their destination. The silent journey lasted maybe thirty minutes and ended in the only small industrial area just outside of Angeles. There were many industries – tire shops and the like, and right at the end of a long and secluded service road sat a row of lockable garages for rent. Many looked derelict and deserted. As they parked up Charlie glanced around to make sure they were alone.

Two large padlocks secured the metal shutters.

"Here, open up the locks.'

He threw a set of keys at Maxwell who failed to catch it, but picked it up and moved towards the door. Charlie stood back, checking the area. The nearest factory building looked about five hundred yards down the straight road.

Maxwell finished opening the padlocks and swung the steel door outwards. The rusty frame scraped on the gravel until it jammed against the ground, open about a third of the way – plenty of room.

Packages the size of a shoe box rested against the walls, all neatly wrapped with brown paper and sealed with duct tape.

"What's this, Charlie?" inquired Maxwell.

The gangster ignored the question. He was busy opening the tailgate of the SUV.

"Pile it all in. It will all go in if we use the seats as well."

Maxwell guessed that he was looking at a fortune in drugs, but these bundles were not drugs.

He took two at a time, taking just ten minutes to fill the car. He filled the tailgate and put a few packs on the back seat. The last few bundles had to be pushed tight up against the back seats to balance out the load. Maxwell leaned deep into the open hatch to wedge the bundles into position.

Charlie crept up silently behind him, unnoticed; until it was too late. Maxwell leaned forward into the car; his hands outstretched in front of him tidying the bundles. Suddenly, he felt a tremendous thud on his lower back, as if a ton weight had fallen from the sky and hit him hard. In fact, Charlie had brought down the hatch of the car on the unsuspecting man with all his might. The gangster may have a problem with his leg, but his upper body and arms were as strong as ever.

Charlie heard the crunch of splitting bone with satisfaction; the tailgate had broken Maxwell's back. He looked around to check that no one could see, then lifted the metal off. The man flailed his arms and groaned in agony, unable to raise himself up - three of his lumbar vertebrae were smashed. Excruciating pain coursed through his limp body as Charlie lifted his protruding legs and tugged the dying man the few yards from the car into the now empty space. Maxwell's head hit the concrete road with a thump as Charlie inched him towards the open garage. It took a significant effort, and Charlie had to favor his damaged leg, but he managed to pull the gasping man through the doorway and into the garage.

Maxwell gurgled, but did not speak; the impact of the car door had also forced a rib into his right lung, now filling with blood. He gasped for breath.

Charlie pulled him into the center of the garage. Maxwell winced as Charlie rolled him over to expose his chest and abdomen. He took Tony's knife from his pocket and wound a cloth around the handle. He was careful not to leave prints on the knife, the only prints any investigators would find would be Tony's. He positioned the blade under Maxwell's third rib to pierce the man's heart and finish him. Their eyes met as Charlie pushed the blade through the shirt and flesh. Maxwell groaned weakly one last time and then was silent. Charlie watched as the life drained out of the poor boy and the limp body became still, Maxwell's eyes remained open, but now fixed, unseeing, on the ceiling.

Charlie closed the door but did not lock it; he picked up the two heavy padlocks and put them in the car. After he'd bombed the hotel with Paul in it, he'd leave the locks at the hotel, to link Tony to that death as well. It was an insurance policy to make sure Tony would never show his face in Angeles again. That was what Charlie wanted.

Charlie glanced at the uniform brown packages filling the car. They could be drugs, but they were not. They were money. Pure and simple. Each package contained half a million US dollars. In the few short years, he'd amassed more than a hundred million dollars. The family had wondered why they did not seem to make the money they should, but he covered his tracks well, and no one even considered blaming the boss's son.

There was a fish restaurant on the way back. 'Isda' was famous for its Tilapia. They'd suspended the tables and walkways on platforms above ponds full of fish. Up to now he'd kept a low profile; someone might see him and report back to his dad, but with Xi dead, and Michael away, he didn't have to worry about that. He felt free for the first time in a long while.

***

Linda was having a break. She took a coffee in her room before the start of the dinner service. Paul left earlier on business and would not be back until late evening. When she noticed Charlie's number come up on his phone, she was relieved that Paul was not around. She had to sort out this situation; it would be much better if Paul never had to learn about Charlie.

"Hello, Charlie. How's your leg?"

"It's fine sweetheart, but never mind about that now. I need to see you. Get a taxi and come to Isda. You know where that is?"

"Yes, give me thirty minutes – I'm on my way."

She'd never be able to break things off with Charlie. She'd seen firsthand how he'd reacted whenever he didn't get his own way. He would likely kill her, and Paul. She had to find another way.

The popular restaurant was beginning to fill when the tricycle dropped her outside. Charlie sat in the far corner, away from most of the diners. He waved and rose as she entered. She noticed he was still a little unsteady on his feet, but he looked well. As she sat down, a waitress brought a bottle of wine that Charlie ordered earlier. He poured two glasses as she settled herself.

"Are we celebrating something?" She smiled, with difficulty. "We certainly are sweetheart." He put a glass into her hand.

"From today everything will be plain sailing, you'll see. We'll get away tomorrow and we'll never have to look back."

She tried her hardest not to look startled.

"Where are we going, Charlie? and what will we do?"

Charlie mistook her panic for surprise.

"It's ok, sweetheart. You'll never have to work again."

Linda continued her efforts to smile.

"Take a look out the window sweet-heart."

Linda followed his gaze through the panoramic window to the car park. Charlie had parked it in a prominent place where he might keep an eye on it.

"Look at the black SUV. Can you see the bundles stacked up in the back? That's money sweetheart. Hundreds of millions of U.S. dollars. More than enough to start again ten times over.

"Where did you get it Charlie? Whoever you robbed will come after us."

"No one will miss it, sweetheart. I've been saving it up for a few years. I've kept it hidden and just collected it this morning." Linda was puzzled.

"How did you put all the packages in the car? You can hardly walk?"

"It's okay, I had some help."

"So, there's at least one other person who knows about this. What if they come after us to steal the money, or run to your dad and tell him?"

Charlie reached over the table and held her hand. He'd have to tell her the truth, that there were no loose ends for anyone to find. She'd understand. It had to be done.

"Yes, I had help to load it up. I asked Maxwell to come with me, but of course, I couldn't let him live after he'd seen that – it would ruin our future if this got out." "You killed him?" He squeezed her hand.

"Hey, keep your voice down. I did it for us. I

didn't want us to start a new life looking over our shoulders, but don't worry, I've made sure someone else will get the blame – there's nothing to link me with Maxwell."

Linda's mind was in a whirl, she thought about Maria, left with small children. How could she have ever loved this monster?

"Well what about your father? He won't give up looking for you; and one day he'll find you."

"That will never happen sweetheart. You remember I had to make a trip to Manila. I needed to meet with my dad. I tried to reason with him, but he wouldn't listen. He's never supported me or had any faith in me. I had no choice sweetheart. He had to go; it was the only way."

"Are you telling me you've killed your father as well?"

Linda was now trying to control her growing hysteria. She was sat here with a madman. Fighting a rising fear, she realized that she had to get away without Charlie suspecting. She had to play along with him, at least for a while.

"Of course. You had no choice, Charlie. But we can put all this behind us now, can't we?"

"Yes, sweetheart. I've just one more little job to do and we will be on our way tomorrow. I want you to come round later this evening. Bring anything you want to take with you. We won't be coming back here. You can stay the night with me at Maxwell's house – there's nobody else there, then we can set off early tomorrow."

Charlie became relaxed. pleased she was taking it this way; he'd worried about how she would react.

"I knew you'd understand. But things will close in soon – we need to get away. Come back around ten, you can stay there while I tend to the last piece of business."

Although frightened, she had to ask, she had to know.

"What is it you have to do tonight, sweetheart?"

There was no harm in telling her now. She'd support him whatever he did.

"That's why I want you away from the hotel tonight. After the shame and disgrace I've suffered in this town, I have to deal with Paul before I go; and I don't want you at the hotel when it happens. I need people to realize they can't cross me and get away with it. I will kill Paul tonight."

Control of her expressions and emotions was getting even more difficult, but she saw that if Charlie suspected what was going through her thoughts, he'd probably kill her too. Charlie rose.

"Go and pack your stuff sweetheart. Try to relax. Angeles will soon be an awful memory for both of us."

Linda waved down a passing taxi. Her mind was made up now. There was no other way.

***

When Charlie got back to Maxwell's house, he took one bundle of the money and brought it into the kitchen, locking the door behind him. He slit it open with a knife and took out a wedge of about one hundred thousand dollars, the rest of the package, he hid in the inside a cabinet. He'd only just had time to pour himself a drink when Tony arrived carrying a large brown paper bag, Charlie opened the door.

"Is that the explosives?" Charlie asked, as Tony put the bag down on the table.

"It sure is. It's stable, but don't put it near any naked flames until you're ready to light it. I've fixed them with short fuses. Ten seconds. We don't want to give him a chance to throw it back at you, do we?" Charlie nodded.

"Come and have a drink, Tony."

Both men sat down at the table. Charlie poured both of them a large whiskey.

"Tony, this is my last night here. I'll be gone tomorrow. I can't give you your knife back – I left it in Maxwell. He's in a lock-up garage – here's the address."

Charlie passed a piece of paper over to him.

"Get his body and dispose of it a bit more permanently."

Tony nodded

Charlie reached into the cupboard for the bundle of dollars and put them in front of Tony.

"I'll call for you as soon as I'm settled. I'll need you to set up a fresh team, and things will not be too good for you here working under Michael." Tony nodded.

"This is to keep you going for a week or two – there's plenty more of that, so make sure you come up and join me when I call you."

"Are you sure you don't want me to help you tonight, Charlie. There might be trouble."

"No, thanks, Tony. I can handle this myself, and it's personal. I want to do this alone."

***

On the way back to the hotel Linda considered her situation. Did she have the strength to go through with it? She reflected on the things her evil boyfriend had done. Yes, she did.

The restaurant was busy as she came through, but she had no time to stop and help. She ran straight to her room and locked the door.

The phone rang several times before a familiar female voice answered.

"Hello, Maria speaking."

Linda breathed heavily with relief. Maria was still alive; Charlie hadn't killed her.

"Maria, this is Linda at the hotel. Where are you?"

"I'm with my mom. I couldn't stand being in the house while Charlie was there, so I came away until he's gone. Maxwell can look after the wicked man."

Linda had a deep sorrow inside. It would not be easy to tell her.

"Maria. I need to meet you urgently. Can you come to the hotel? Paul isn't here."

"Sure, give me thirty minutes and I'll be there."

Linda tidied the room and had a pot of coffee sent in and waited anxiously for her friend downstairs. She did not have to wait long. Maria bustled in looking anxious.

"What's wrong dear? What is it that you could not tell me over the phone?"

"Come up to my room, Maria. It's more private there."

They climbed the stairs in silence, neither of them spoke until they were sat nursing their coffees.

"Linda, why all the cloak and dagger stuff.

What is it you have to tell me?"

"It's about Charlie..., and Maxwell."

"Okay, Linda, tell me what's going on. I can't wait any longer."

"Well, it turns out that Charlie had a hidden stash of cash – an enormous amount, and he plans of running off with it, and with me. He fetched it this afternoon. Maxwell helped him to load the money into his car."

Maria was listening intently and nodding – Linda took a deep breath.

"Maria, Charlie killed Maxwell to stop him telling anyone about the money. I'm so sorry Maria – Maxwell is dead."

What else could she say. She reached out and held the shocked Maria's hand.

"I'm so sorry, my dear, and I'm sorry to tell you so quickly and so bluntly, but there are other things going on that we have to deal with right now. I had to let you know straight away."

For a long time, Maria just stared at Linda, open mouthed. Eventually she spoke.

"Maxwell can't be dead. I spoke to him yesterday – he was fine."

"Maria, this is difficult, and I know it's a great shock. But you have to accept it. You must consider yourself and the kids now. I'll help you, but you need to know situation. We have things to do to protect ourselves for the future. Do you understand?"

Maria nodded through her sobs.

"Oh, Linda, what am I gonna do? We rent the house, and we have two young kids."

"Maria, it's very difficult, and I can't imagine what you're going through, but you and I need to work together to prevent even more atrocities. If we get this right, we should all be okay. You've got to think of your kids now."

Maria was crying, holding her head in her hands.

"I realized that man would bring us trouble. I warned Maxwell but he wouldn't listen to me. I wish I'd killed that Charlie when I had the chance. I had plenty of opportunity when he was still weak and at my house."

"Please listen, Maria. There's something else I must tell you. When I met Charlie earlier, he said he wanted me to stay at your house with him tonight because he was coming here to kill Paul. He plans to blow up the hotel. I can't allow that to happen, Maria. I love Paul, I want Charlie out of our lives forever."

She looked up at Maria who was concentrating on her words despite her tears.

"Maria, there is only one answer. Charlie must die. I can't do it by myself, but we have to kill him. I can do it with your help. Will you help me?"

Maria continued to sob, but after a few seconds she nodded.

"Of course, I will. I want that bastard dead." "Okay, Maria. I've got a plan. Here's what we'll do…"

***

Streetlights were just coming on as the dusk approached. As the tricycle took her round the corner into Maxwell's road, she saw Maria's car parked up out of sight of her house.

Linda alighted from the tricycle and took her case from the rack. Taking a deep breath, she pulled it along the path to Maxwell's front door, it was already ajar. She walked straight in and was met by a smiling Charlie sat at the kitchen table with a large glass of whiskey. Linda was pleased to see this. It may make things go better.

"That's not a very big case. I thought you'd have a lot more than that."

"I've never had much of my own Charlie. I've got everything I need."

Charlie rose from his seat, but he still winced, his leg was taking longer to heal because he hadn't rested it. Linda moved over to him. "Here, let me help you. Perhaps I should redress the wound."

Charlie nodded gratefully and Linda helped him through onto the bed.

"Would you like some more whiskey while I take care of it, just in case there's some pain?" "That would be nice, sweetheart. Thank you."

Linda passed through to get the hot water and bandages, and the whiskey.

She came back through and unwound the dressing. There was no blood now so only a minor discomfort. When she got it all off, she looked at the dry scar.

"That's healing nicely, nearly mended now."

She gingerly touched around the scar. It didn't seem to cause him any problems. She stroked his leg smiling at him. When her hand slid up to his testicles she reached inside and cupped him.

"Are you okay for this?"

She smiled as she held his growing penis with her other hand.

"I certainly am, sweetheart. It's been a long time."

"Well, that will make it even more special. You lay down, I'll get on top of you. Don't worry, I'll do all the work."

She helped him to lay flat, putting a pillow under his head. He didn't question why she had him lie at the bottom of the bed with his head pointing towards the open door.

"Let me make you more comfortable."

He raised himself from the bed with a little discomfort so she could slide his pants down. Charlie was getting excited now but was not yet fully erect. She saw what she had to do.

"This is what you need, sweetheart."

She smiled up at his as she guided him into her mouth. It was all mechanical. She'd done it many times before. She noted that

Paul was bigger than him as a passing thought. Charlie moaned contentedly, lost in the moment as his girlfriend swallowed him deeply.

Linda was wearing a short skirt she usually wore for work, so she lifted it around her waist. She always wore a thong when she met Charlie, and she thought she had better do so tonight. The tiny piece of white cotton fell to the floor. She sat astride him now with her legs wide open. She'd shaved especially. Charlie's erection told her he appreciated the blow job and the strip tease.

Linda moved up on Charlie's prone body and rubbed the head of him against her opening. There was little moisture there yet, and she didn't want any discomfort.

As she rubbed him up and down, in front of her, in the doorway, she saw the shadow. Maria was there, waiting to do her part. Linda groaned for effect as she rubbed Charlie's fully stiff cock up and down along the moistening slit between her legs until gently, she impaled herself on him with a sigh. His eyes were closed with ecstasy as she slid fully down onto him.

"Oh, Charlie, that's nice. Fuck me harder."

That was Maria's cue. While Linda was bouncing up and down on the spellbound Charlie, Maria sneaked up behind his head. Maria was a nurse. A head shot would be quickest and cleanest, but she wanted this evil man to suffer. She aimed carefully. The first bullet hit his lower abdomen about six inches above Linda's vagina. The second shot was higher up and to the left. It would shatter his liver. It would take him about twenty minutes to die in agony.

His eyes were wide open now and his mouth gaping like a fish.

"Oh my god. What have you done?"

Linda slowly slid off his flagging penis and put her clothes back on.

Maria had shot him in the lower spine to make sure he couldn't move. She came round to face him now.

"You deserve this, you bastard. In fact, you deserve worse. Maxwell was a weak man, but he didn't deserve to die – and certainly not at your hands."

Charlie was still wide-eyed, and now unable to speak, he could only gurgle.

Linda moved to the kitchen and came back with a large knife.

"Did you ever think I, or anyone else for that matter, would ever be ok with what you've done. I hate you Charlie, and you would never marry me because you're already married. I'm with Paul now, and I will not let anything impede that. The world is better off without you, and to think I had to let you fuck me again today. I haven't finished hurting you yet, you evil man."

Linda lifted his limp penis and stretched it. In three deep sawing motions the dripping member was in her hand, and the stump was pumping blood out. She knew it would end his life sooner, but she had to do it.

Maria came further in and put an arm on her shoulder. Charlie's eyes were glazing now, but he was still breathing, shallowly.

"What are we going to do now, just hang around and wait for him to die?"

"No, we can get on with our plan even if he's still breathing. There's nothing he can do."

Maria backed her estate wagon up as close to the house as she could so they wouldn't have far to carry Charlie – there was just two meters between the door and the empty wagon.

They rolled Charlie over and then rolled him up in the sheet – he'd be easier to carry that way. They took one end each and pulled him out of the bedroom and lifted him up into the back of the car in one action. He was still alive, but shaking now, Loss of blood was causing shock to set in. "Can you remember where you used to take Joe?" Maria asked.

"Oh yes, I know where to go,"

The path up into the mountains was winding, and little traveled, the further up they got. After about forty minutes they reached the end of the track. and pulled off into the bush. They eased the limp, but still breathing body out of the trunk and dumped it into the gorse bushes. Many needles and spikes perforated Charlie's body, but that was the least of his worries. He was fading in and out of consciousness, but he saw Maria's red station wagon pull away and head back down the hill.

Something nudged against his leg and turned his head around. A large black pig was nudging at the wound on his calf.

Animals always chose any damaged parts first. There was a searing pain as the old boar sank his teeth into his leg and tugged a long strip off.

***

Maria drove slowly back to her house in a daze; she was still in shock. Linda sat beside her crying. They both needed to sort themselves out before they could face the world. The black car with all the money in was parked on the drive, so they parked up on the road in front of the house and hurried through to the kitchen, closing the door to the bloody bedroom on the way. Maria saw the half empty bottle of whiskey on the table and threw it in the bin. She wanted nothing that Charlie had touched.

She took a fresh bottle and two clean glasses from the cupboard.

"Have some of this. I think we both need it."

Linda didn't object. On the drainer, Linda spotted a set of car keys.

"Are those Charlie's keys?"

"I guess they must be, they're not mine."

The girls stared at each other and drank more whiskey. It was ten p.m. before Linda staggered outside and flagged down a tricycle to take her back to the hotel. As she entered, she noted, with relief, that Paul was not yet home. She needed a shower before she could face him.

Refreshed, she put on one of her best dresses to meet him and waited in the bar area nursing another whiskey. Paul came in about eleven p.m. and was surprised to find her sitting there.

"I thought you'd be in bed, sweetheart. Why are you waiting up?"

Her head rolled over towards him.

"I missed you, sweetheart, I wanted to be here when you returned."

He smiled and lifted her head.

"I think you've had one too many drinks today – is there as special occasion?'

"Yes, there is. I love you Paul, and I want to marry you. No more sneaking around now. Let's tell the staff tomorrow that we're a couple. We can get married as soon as your divorce comes through."

Paul smiled like a Cheshire cat and lifted her to her feet so he could embrace her. Their kiss was passionate and long-lasting. Paul had to carry her up the stairs to bed. He did so willingly.

***

Next day, for the first time they could remember, Linda did not come down to take charge of the breakfast service, but it was ok – they weren't too busy.

The staff smiled, however, when Paul and Linda came down at ten a.m. holding hands and smiling. There had been rumours, but now they knew for sure.

The happy couple didn't say anything – they didn't need to. They sat closely together while staff served breakfast and coffees to them.

Paul kissed her, not caring who was watching.

"I'm going to the lawyer, sweetheart. It will be a couple of months before we can marry, so I want to transfer the hotel to our joint names. I want you to know I'm serious about you, about us. You've made me happier than I've ever been in my life. I don't want to lose you, ever."

"Oh, that's so sweet, Paul. You don't have to do that, but I appreciate the gesture."

"It's fine, sweetheart. I want you to feel secure. I'm meeting some friends for lunch too, so I'll see you this afternoon.

They kissed once more before Paul left.

Yesterday was a stressful day to say the least. Linda suddenly felt tired and decided to go upstairs for a rest.

As she lay down on the bed her phone rang. It was Maria.

"I just wanted to check on you, how are you today?"

"Well, surprisingly, Maria, I feel good, maybe a little sore" Maria giggled.

"Things went well with Paul, then?"

"It certainly did. We are officially a couple now. We'll get married as soon as we can."

"Wonderful news. Linda, I'm so happy for you. Can we meet for a coffee? I'm not sure when I'll be going away, or when I will be back."

"Yes sure, Maria, that would be nice. Where shall we meet?"

"Actually, I'm right outside your hotel, so, shall I come in?"

Linda laughed.

"Of course, come on in. I'll have some coffee sent up – you know where my room is – come on up."

The coffee was hot and steaming when Maria came into the room carrying a plastic bag which she put down beside the table. The girls smiled and embraced. Linda looked into Maria's eyes.

"How are you today? Yesterday must have been so bad for you."

"Yes, I know. But I think I'm coming to terms with it. I loved Maxwell, but he was a stupid boy, easily influenced. I was always worried about what he would get up to next. My kids are very young. They've already stopped asking about him. As for getting rid of Charlie. It was a job that had to be done."

Linda nodded.

"How about you?" asked Maria. "It was a hell of a day for you as well." Linda smiled.

"Don't worry about me. I'm sorry for your loss, of course, but I'm sure you'll make a new, better life. We have to remember, dear, the whole world is better off without Charlie – especially Angeles."

The two sipped their coffee, they had grown closer over the events of the last twenty-four hours.

"Will you stay with your parents now, Maria?"

"No, I need a complete break. I'll go somewhere different, where I'm not known. When we're out of Angeles I'll buy a new car and dump this one. I don't want any traces, any links."

"Yes. That's the best thing to do. What's in the bag? It looks like you've been shopping."

Maria picked the large package up and put it on the table.

"A little present for you."

Linda raised her eyebrows and opened the bag. Inside was one of the neatly wrapped bundles of money.

"I know you'll be able to put that to good use, Linda. I did a lot of thinking last night. There was a car filled with money sat on my drive, and Charlie owed us – it's not theft, it's only right. We deserve that for what he did to us."

Linda put down the bundle, tears welled in her eyes; she didn't know what to say.

"Don't thank me Linda, you've more than earned it. You came from a poor family, like me. Let's use this to spread some warmth, some happiness, that way it'll help us both feel more okay about the whole thing. We can put it behind us then."

Linda was crying now.

"Oh, Maria, thank you so much. My family can certainly use the help."

After Maria left, Linda opened the bag. Inside were one hundred bundles of American dollars – about US$100,000 – she'd never seen so much money before, and probably never would again.

Linda often sent parcels to her mom, so she had a supply of wrapping paper and tape beside her wardrobe.

She made four neat equal piles, then put them on the floor to clear the table. Carefully, she wrapped the first bundle, she wrote a brief note to put inside it.

'Hi Mom, I hope you and dad are well. This is to make your life a little easier. Don't tell dad about it, he'll waste it. Use what you need and save the rest in a secret place. It should take care of any medical emergencies there may be, oh, and get the roof fixed. Last time I came, the rain came through and dripped on me while I was sleeping. I'll come and see you soon. I love you x.'

She sealed the parcel and addressed it; onto the next one.

She prepared the package in the same way, then wrote another note.

'Jinky, you won't believe what's been happening here. It's been a nightmare, but it's all over now. Charlie's not a problem anymore, and I'm with Paul now. I hope you can come and see us sometime, but if you do, don't mention this money. Paul doesn't know about it. Call it 'compensation' and don't ask where it came from, Love, Love, Linda.'

Two down, two to go. Linda lifted one pile of money and hid it at the back of the wardrobe in her room. It was safe there; she was the only one who ever went there. She packed up the final bundle, she seemed to take more care over this one. Just before sealing she put a note with just one word on it. *'Sorry.'* She stuck a label on the top and addressed it to the parents of the young kitchen lad she'd killed.

Linda looked at her watch; she just had time to go to the FedEx Office before Paul came back. She couldn't trust parcels like this to the local postal service.

By now Maria was an hour outside of Angeles. She looked at the disappearing buildings in her rear-view mirror and wondered if she'd ever see them again. The two children were fast asleep in the new baby seats in the back, with brown paper bundles stacked either side of them.

She headed down the Northern Luzon

Express way in the general direction of Manila but she knew she would not end up there. To her right would be Pangasinan with its beaches and fishponds, to her left would be Batangas, famous for coffee and an extinct volcano.

For a brief second, she wished Maxwell was with her. How her world had turned on its head in twenty-four hours. *'Lyin' eyes'* came on the radio: she smiled and started to sing along.

About the Author

Arthur Crandon If you enjoyed this book, you can do the author a GREAT favour by leaving a review on Amazon.

Arthur Crandon has been voted **No. 1 by Goodreads** readers in their poll – 'Little known authors worth reading'.

He writes thrillers, suspense, and intrigue novels, mainly set in South-East Asia.

Arthur is a former British lawyer who worked in the UK, Hong Kong and the Philippines, specializing in visas and immigration – a great source of inspiration for his stories. His time as a warden for the British Embassy in Manila also provided insight for his writing. In between writing and blogging.

He has an M. A. in creative writing and plans further study after that. In his spare time, he enjoys music (he is a keyboards player) and cooking. Arthur is married with five children.

Contact Arthur Crandon

You can keep up with his work and contact him at the links below:

Website: http://www.arthurcrandon.com

Blog: http://www.arthurcrandon.com/blogblogblog.html

Facebook: facebook.com/ArthurCrandonAuthor

Twitter: http://www.twitter.com/arthurcrandon

Pinterest: http://pinterest.com/arFFthurcrandon

If you liked the book, please leave a review online, and to contact the author, please email him at ac@arthurcrandon.com.

Other books by Arthur Crandon

Arthur's first novel set in the Philippines. *Deadly Election* is like no other thriller that you will ever read.

There is nothing more frightening than a man that will do anything for power and riches. Paul McCain is on a mission to stop an evil and corrupt politician from ruling the Philippines – will he succeed? Or will the vicious crook 'deal' with him. It's not your everyday thriller – find out for yourself.

hyperurl.co/DEADLYELECTION

You will not regret it.

#Thriller #MustRead

This first book in Arthur's series of ghosts, apparitions, and other evil creatures which send chills into the hearts of everyday folk. *Bloodline Curse* is the well-known story of a half-man, half-snake monster, born to a nobleman. It lives in the basement of a shopping mall and lives on young girl shoppers until someone can kill it. It does not end well for the Governor and his family.

Find out for yourself here:
geni.us/BLOODLINECURSE

Continuing the series of ghostly legends, Arthur writes about the
Santilmo, a sentient and deadly Fireball which arises to avenge
wrongful deaths.
It will track down the evildoers and try to make amends.
This book is set in the second world war and involves atrocities
committed by the Jap. Invaders of helpless villagers.
Many people believe these avengers exist – make your own mind up:
geni.us/SANTILMO